i

A Season for All Things

Larry Parmeter

Pocol Press

POCOL PRESS
Published in the United States of America
by Pocol Press
6023 Pocol Drive
Clifton, VA 20124
www.pocolpress.com

Publisher's Cataloguing-in-Publication

Names: Parmeter, Larry, author.
Title: A Season for all things / Larry Parmeter
Description: Clifton, VA: Pocol Press, 2017.
Identifiers: ISBN 978-1-929763-74-0 | LCCN 2017939518
Subjects: LCSH Widowers--Fiction. | United States--Description and travel--Fiction. | Grief—Fiction.
| Travelers--Fiction. | Secrets--Fiction. | Family--Fiction. | Friendship--Fiction. | Man-woman relationships--Fiction. | BISAC FICTION / General.
Classification: LCC PS3616 .A7575 S43 2017 | DDC 813.6--dc23

Library of Congress Control Number: 2017939518

To everything there is a season, and a time to every purpose under heaven; a time to be born, and a time to die, a time to plant and a time to pluck what is planted; a time to kill and a time to heal; a time to break down and a time to build up; a time to weep, and a time to laugh; a time to mourn and a time to dance; a time to cast away stones, and a time to gather stones together; a time to embrace, and a time to refrain from embracing; a time to lose, and a time to get; a time to keep and a time to cast away; a time to rend, and a time to sew; a time to keep silent and a time to speak; a time to love and a time to hate, a time of war and a time of peace…

Ecclesiastes 3:1-8

To my son Nathan Sean, the most blessed gift a parent can have; and to my father, the late John Parmeter, who taught me to examine life in all its enlightenment and grace.

Table of Contents

Prologue

We buried Beatrice on March 7. She had endured for three years and was now finally sleeping, away from the misery, the needles, the chemo, the scarring. With Danae on one side of me and Laura on the other, I watched as the urn holding her ashes was lowered into the soft damp ground speckled with sunlight, and then covered up with spades of dirt. Eventually, a marker would go there, but not yet.

I walked back to the limo where the driver in his black suit and cap were waiting. I did not look back at the mound. There would be time for that later. Instead, I eased myself into the back seat, while Danae took the space in front and Laura sat beside me, holding my hand. What fine daughters Beatrice and I had produced, both successful, and now steady and assured in the first major family tragedy of their adult lives. Even with all of the outstanding students that had gone through my classroom over the years, I could not have asked for two better children. They had been Beatrice's posts since the illness hit, and now they were my posts, and I could not ask for anything more from them.

The vehicle moved silently though the clear watery air of the cemetery, past new graves, old graves, and graves yet to be. Beatrice's oldest brother was here, as well as my mother; today's ceremony was, in a sense, a family gathering of both the living and the dead, as if they were initiating another member into a society which we would all eventually join one way or another. And we weren't the only ones. Our neighbors, the Sangers, also had pending membership here, as did the Dowds, whom I knew from school. The papers and cards were already being processed.

As we left, the shadows of the trees swirling in and out of the car's windows, I thought about what my life would be like from now on. At least up to a few months ago, Beatrice and I had been trying to live a more or less normal existence, as well as we could with her condition. Getting up, going to work, sharing breakfasts and dinners, weekends in the mountains or at the beach, or quietly talking over the gurgle of the pond in the backyard while the sun sunk slowly over the houses around us, the trees swaying in the evening breezes, as if attempting to capture our conversations. Now, that was ended, and I would return to a house that still had the appearance of Beatrice: her clothes, books, blankets, hairbrushes and combs, coffee cups, hats, shoes, coats, and all the other artifacts.

1

But the form, the essence that completed them, that made them more than simply store-bought physical objects, was no longer around. The slight sag in the folding chair on the back porch, the kitchen chair where she always sat, and especially the right side of the bed that we shared would no longer be filled with what was her. There was only the memory that completed them.

After the ceremony at the cemetery, I faced the reception at the house. With a few exceptions, people were distantly polite, saying how sorry they were, then moving off to chat with friends and eat from the buffet that Laura had ordered. She had also arranged for a service to come and clean the house so that the antiseptic smell was mostly gone. Maybe because I had been around it so much lately, I still picked it up, as if it, like tobacco smoke, had indelibly filtered into the furniture and walls and become a part of the structure itself. At one point, I tentatively entered our bedroom, where Beatrice had died six days before. I had not been in it since that day, spending the time at Laura's house in Fresno. The bed had been made up, the nightstand was clear of medications, the rug cleaned and vacuumed, the closets closed, the clothes chest dusted and polished. The room looked like a model home display, yet I knew it was something else. It was the room where Beatrice and I had made our pact of life, where our daughters had been conceived and where on many Saturday and Sunday mornings they woke us from sleep. It was where I told Beatrice that I had been hired at the high school, where she told me that a publisher had accepted her first novel, both events that marked turning points in our lives. It was also where, one afternoon when I got home from school, she informed me of the visit to the doctor's office and the suspicious "spot" in one of her breasts that turned our destinies onto the path that ended at the cemetery earlier in the day. I left the room and closed the door.

Back in the living room and the rest of the house, the reception was diminishing. People who had been trying to find me now expressed their best wishes, sincerely, or so I hoped, and made their way out. I could hear the opening and closing of car doors in the front, the starting of engines, and the pulling away from the curbs on both sides of the street. Laura came up to me. Refusing to wear black that day, she had on a beige skirt and jacket with ivory white blouse that suited her so well, making her look years older and far more mature than the twenty five that she was.

"Dad, do you want to stay here tonight, or come back to the house?"

"If you don't mind, I'll stay at your place again tonight, and start moving back here tomorrow or maybe Friday. Honey, you've done so much already, I don't want to impose on you anymore."

"Dad, it's no problem at all. You're welcome at my place anytime, and stay as long as you want."

"No, I've got to get back to something resembling a normal life, and the longer I put it off, the harder it'll be. I just told Barbara Winston I'll be back in the classroom on Monday. She's just said, 'Take all the time you need,' but I've got to return to a routine or I'll go crazy."

"Ok. Just tell me when you want to leave here."

"I don't know. I've never done this before. I think I'm supposed to stay until everyone else is gone." And she and I smiled together for the first time in weeks.

On Monday morning I was back in my classroom, surrounded by Jefferson, Washington, Einstein, Hitler, Churchill, Kennedy, and Reagan. Not really them, of course, but posters hanging on the walls to remind me of the profession that I was in; that, like all other things, they, too, were dead, but life goes on.

I made myself settle into my old companion of a swivel desk chair and glanced at the notes and plans left by the young woman who had been my sub for the past two weeks. Each day that I was gone was marked by neatly stacked with papers and quizzes-ungraded-and a summary of that day's events. George Melendez was sent to the office again for talking back; Amy Campole received a note from her mother to go home in the middle of the test on World War I, she hasn't yet finished making it up; Stacy Lopez got sick and went to the nurse; and so on. I put them aside to deal with later, and rubber-banded the assignments and stuck them in a desk drawer. Maybe if they stayed there long enough, they would grade themselves or maybe even disappear. I studied the roll sheets. The usual number absent on test day; the other times, only one or two missing per class, not too bad. On the other hand, a number of sympathy cards and letters were scattered all over the desk, some from colleagues, most from students. Somehow, thinking back, these kids were screw-ups, lazy, unmotivated, wanting the easy way out on everything, but in a real issue, a real defining moment, their comments were warm and sincere, ...*Mr. Lindstrom, I can't even imagine how it would feel to lose someone I was with for so many years...Mr. Lindstrom, I hope she didn't suffer too much, and died very peacefully...I hope you love and remember her as much as I remember my grandmother who died two years ago...*after a while I couldn't read any more and put them aside for another time.

The rest of that first day back went in slow motion, *Groundhog Day*-like images. The bell ringing, students coming up and saying how

3

sorry they were, my reviewing what they had done while I was gone, an explication of readings and assignments for the rest of the semester, and a summing up of my thanks for cooperation with the sub and turning in their assignments, which I promised them I'd grade and return as soon as I could. Then the final bell of the day rang at 3:15, and I sat back in the chair, drained and exhausted.

It went on more or less like that the next day and for the rest of the week, and into the remainder of April and into May. My AP class took its test and then relaxed for a few days, and the others continued with the Cold War and the Watergate Affair up through the Gulf War and the downfall of the Soviet Union. Then it was June and a summing up of the New Millennium and America's prospects in the twenty-first century. All the while I wrote dozens of thank-you cards to people, and opened the windows and the doors at every opportunity. Eventually the house began to smell less of medicines and flowers and more of potted plants, breakfast cereal, and dirty laundry, the way it used to be.

I also slept in the guestroom. I just couldn't bring myself to sleep in the room where Beatrice and I had spent the nights of our lives. The fact that she died in that room didn't bother me; it was the idea that she lived there for so long that I found uncomfortable. I still felt her presence there, under the sheets, on the pillows, over the mattress, almost everywhere in there while I dispiritedly tried to sort through a lifetime of her possessions. As a result, the bed and the floor slowly filled up with piles of books, writings, towels, blankets, scarves, hats, jackets, shirts, skirts, dresses, pants, shoes: all reminders of my wife who once was. Eventually, I moved most of my clothes and personal items over to the guestroom.

I still kept wondering, though, where do I go from here? Beatrice and I had been together for 30 years if the time before getting married was thrown in. That was over half my life with one person, and now I was the one person left. The insurance statistics said that the wife usually outlived the husband by about five years, but the statistics didn't take into account the deadly cells accumulating in the female body, cells that would disrupt not only the life of the carrier, but the lives of everyone else around her. Somehow, as it always seemed to happen, real life didn't follow the numbers, and instead flung off on trajectories of its own, leaving untold carnage in its wake, damage that would take a lifetime to clean up, and even when the visible wreckage was gone, the spots and the odors still remained, reminders of what once was and would never completely be eliminated.

In the evenings, if I had time, I walked over to the Fresno River that bisected the town. The term "river" is a misnomer, since the

4

riverbed is totally dry and has been for a great number of years. I wandered along a path that paralleled the dusty bank in the dusk, while rabbits and ground squirrels scurried out of the way, and considered my condition. I had no ready answers despite the fact that I should have been preparing for this. But while Beatrice was still alive I considered that almost treasonous, turning against the one that I loved and, in a sense, making plans behind her back. I was numbed, almost afraid to strike out and move forward. Only later did I realize that I, too, was in pain, and like the figures in Greek tragedy, had to live with it in order to remind me what had happened.

All that spring, while I toiled at the stubborn stains of the memories that made up our relationship, I kept thinking what would Beatrice do in this same situation if I died? She wouldn't waste time going through the accumulated debris of the past, she wouldn't sit around aimlessly, she wouldn't reflect on what we had. She would go out and find the future. To use a cliché, she would look on the bright side of life and move on.

It was not just Beatrice. For the past several years, I had put aside a number of nagging doubts and concerns about issues which were deep in my history, having to do with my family and some of my friends. Our marriage, my daughters, and, above all, the struggle with Beatrice's illness had pushed them all into the shadows. Now that, to put it as nicely as possible, a major crisis in my life had passed, they were returning and seemingly becoming more pressing than ever. I felt that I could not ignore them any longer; Beatrice was gone and the girls were grown up. I had no more excuses or distractions for putting them off.

I continued with my classes, keeping up with the curriculum and the paperwork, but I am sure that the students noted that I was sometimes only dimly aware of them, and what I was doing as well. Every now and then one of them would come up and ask, "Are you okay, Mr. Lindstrom?" I would just give a false smile, and reply that I was fine, but inside, I knew that I wasn't. I was directionless and in turmoil, and it was time to start reassembling my life.

Three weeks before school ended for the year, I went to see the principal, Barbara Winston, or Mrs. Winston. Even though she was four years younger than me, she was still my boss, and I just couldn't think of calling her anything but Mrs. Winston, however, many of my colleagues called her Barbara. I knocked on her door, and, with her always modulated pleasant voice, she called out, "Come in."

"Mrs. Winston, I have a couple of things to ask of you. First of all, is the summer school world history position still open?"

"Yes."

"I'll take it, then."

Her eyes opened in surprise and acceptance. "It's yours. That solves one problem. What's the other thing?"

"I'd like to take off the coming school year. A leave of absence, a sabbatical, whatever term the school district uses for it. I know it's sudden, and probably the last thing you expected, and a pain in the butt in paperwork, but it's something I feel I need to do right now."

Barbara Winston looked at me intently for a minute, and then motioned me to sit down at the chair next to her desk. She was silent for another moment, then slowly replied, "Michael, I know you've just gone through a terrible tragedy, and I just want to make sure you've thought this out enough. Offhand, I've no objections to your request, but I want to make sure it's the right thing for you. You're sure you want to do it?"

"Yes, I've thought this out for some time. It's what I want to do."

"If I may ask, what are you going to do during your time off?"

"I'm going to travel. I'm going to visit family and friends that I haven't seen in a long time. And also, I feel that I just need time away, away from here, nothing personal, time away from everything. Besides, there's a lot of the country that I've never seen, and it's about time that I did, before something happens to me. I'm not running away from anyone or anything, maybe I want to run to something, whatever it might be. I don't know. I do know that I just need to get out, away from the usual routine. That's all."

She nodded, giving her unspoken approval. "But you've got to promise to come back in a year. Otherwise, I'll go looking for you myself and drag you back here, do you understand?" We both smiled.

"I'll be back. That's a guarantee."

"I'll have to find someone to take your place. It won't be easy to hire a person for just a year, and then have to let them go."

"I've already thought about that. I'd like that young woman, Angelica Baronas, the one who subbed for me when I was gone, to take my classes. She did a great job with the kids. Not only that, Joe MacLeod has already said that he's retiring after next year, so she can take his place when I return. She talked to me about it when I came back; she's looking for a full time permanent position."

"You've got this all figured out." She grinned at me. "All right, I'll have to get going on this ASAP. You need to go over to the district office and start filling out the paperwork as soon as you can, like later today. I'll have to do some as well. I'll contact Ms. Baronas. I've heard good things about her as a sub. She'll have to go through the regular hiring process, but that can be taken care of." She suddenly changed

6

direction. "Can you afford to do this, and what about your insurance?"

"I've already gone over my finances, I can do this. To be honest, between my assets and Beatrice's estate and life insurance, I don't have a lot of money problems. I could probably retire right now if I wanted to." She gave me a glare. "But I won't." She smiled. "And I'll talk to the district business office about continuing my health insurance while I'm gone. I might have to pay a bit more for it, but I can handle that."

"What about your two girls?" She was now sounding less like a boss and more like a concerned mother.

"Danae is twenty and in college, and Laura is twenty-five and married. If they can't take care of themselves by now, I don't know when they ever will. They can do without me for a while."

Barbara grinned. "I keep thinking of when they were five and seven. I guess they're not anymore. Even my kids are grown up now. We forget how quickly time passes." She paused. "All right, mothering time is over even if you're older than me. You're a big boy now and can find your own way. If you can't I don't know what we're going to do with you. Go over to the DO right away and start working on this. The sooner the better."

I stood up and walked towards the door. "Thank you, Mrs. Winston."

"Michael," she said, "Good luck, and take care, and come back to us."

7

Interlude One

He left Madera early on a September morning, driving south on Highway 99, crossing the San Joaquin River, passing Fresno, Selma, Kingsburg, then Visalia and Tulare, moving into the Valley with its endless fields of raisin grapes being harvested. He had bought a truck for this trip, a ten year old Toyota mini truck that he felt would do better than his Nissan sedan. For one thing, it had a five speed stick shift instead of an automatic transmission. He had not driven a car with a stick shift since he and Beatrice had married. Beatrice had never learned to drive one. The clutch and shifter felt odd at first since it had been so many years, but he soon adjusted to it, and enjoyed the foot and hand movements after a while. He felt as if he had more control over the vehicle. Both of his daughters thought he was crazy to buy a stick shift. Of course, they thought it absolutely demented that he was going on the trip at all. "Dad, so soon after mom's death. What would she say? And what are you going to do if you have a heart attack or a stroke or something like that?" They cited stories claiming that men often suffer serious illnesses, even die themselves, shortly after the deaths of their spouses, that they can't handle life after their loved ones are gone, and so on. He smiled at them. "Your mother would be pleased if I did something like this. She would want me to. And I'm not that old. You two think that anyone over thirty is destined for the nursing home. I'll be fine." In the end, he did agree to buy an iPhone with GPS and email and nationwide calling service and promised to contact them at least once a week. They, in turn, would look after the house. Danae, in fact, would live at home during her junior year at Merced, commute in Beatrice's Jetta, and take care of the utility bills and the mail while living in the room she had grown up in. "Now, no parties while I'm gone," he told her only half facetiously before he left, "And remember, Charlemagne will tell me everything that happened when I get home." Charlemagne was the big black and white tomcat that showed up on their front porch one morning five years earlier and subsequently announced that he was staying, regardless of what the inhabitants thought. He left money in a special account for emergencies, and arranged to pay whatever other bills he had through his tablet, another alien device he agreed to buy and take with him on the road.

He left with mixed emotions. He would miss the rhythm of life at the high school, the regularity of classes and lessons, the interaction with the students, the personal and intellectual challenge he felt when teaching. In a strange way, he would miss the daily goofiness of the kids, their quirks, their social dramas, their very real anxieties and fears. It would also be the first time he had been away from his two daughters for any extended period. Laura had gone to college locally, at Fresno Pacific, and Danae's college, if not strictly local, was close enough to come home almost every weekend to check on her mother and make sure that he was healthy and stable. There were also friends at church, the local historical society, and other community groups that he participated in. It was not as if he was going away forever, he thought to himself. Yet the patterns of his life were being broken and scattered for the first time in many years.

He thought of how much Beatrice had been a part of this landscape. She, in fact, was grounded in the regional soil and the people, indelibly connected to both. When he first met her at college, she had lived almost her entire life in and around Fresno. She had been born and raised on a farm on the West Side, the second youngest of five children, one of whom took over the family acreage and still cultivated it. With the exception of occasional trips to the coast and visits to Los Angeles and San Francisco, she rarely traveled outside the Central Valley area until she graduated from high school. Then she learned about the larger world and, although she found excitement and stimulation in its offerings, remained faithful to the land of her roots. Eventually, they had met, and he respected her decision to return to the Valley. They were married in a church in Fresno, and after a year of apartment dwelling, bought a house in nearby Madera, where they had lived ever since.

There they settled and began their married lives and careers. He took time to adjust to the more languid pace of the Central Valley, the frustrations of working with students, most of whom considered their main goal to buy cars and get jobs, not to go to college. He remembered his first year at the high school, talking to a girl who wanted to skip an SAT practice session. "My mother was head cheerleader when she was here, my aunt was head cheerleader, and a few years ago, my cousin was head cheerleader. It's always been my dream to be on cheer." He began to realize that Beatrice was a rare bird; she told him that she had wanted to go to college from an early age, and her parents tried to dissuade her. Only she and her younger brother ultimately went beyond high school; their three older siblings were married and had families by the time each was twenty.

Nevertheless, they persevered. He thrived at the high school, and Beatrice found her niche at the junior college. In the evenings, he worked on history projects, and she graded essays. When the girls came along, they adjusted accordingly, and after the success of Beatrice's first book, she was able to go from full-time to part-time. They watched the girls grow and mature, develop their own distinctions, and eventually go

9

off to college. At the same time, they settled easily into middle age married and professional life. Then came the diagnosis.

Now, as he drove south, he thought of his initial route. He would take Highway 99 to Bakersfield, and then head east on Highway 152 through the Tehachapi Mountains down into Mojave, and then, beyond it, connect with Interstate 10 and across the desert to Blythe and beyond. He knew a place on the Colorado River, among the sagebrush and the barren rocks and the desert sky, away from the city, away from the pain.

September

He spent the first night in a small campground on the Arizona side of the River. Across the rolling expanse he could see the lights of Blythe, California, which he had passed through a few hours earlier. Now, in the campground, there were only two other vehicles and himself. Since he wanted privacy he stayed some distance from them, and set up his stove and overhang at a cement table in the mesquite and sagebrush. To save money, he had decided to camp as long as the weather cooperated, and spend time in hotels when it got too cold or wet. While the sun was still up, he cooked a simple dinner of eggs and sausage on the propane stove, and finished it with canned applesauce and cold water. By the time he cleaned up, the sun was just below the horizon, and the quiet winds associated with the desert evening began to pick up. In the far distance, he could hear the sounds of cars on the highway, and in the near vicinity, he picked up the cries of insects and small mammals. As darkness descended, the sky turned from blue to purple, the lights of Blythe became more and more reflected on the river, cirrus clouds drifted far above his head, and one by one stars came out. Within an hour it was dark, and he could feel the chill of the desert night on his skin. In the air, he heard the hoot of a Great Horned Owl somewhere along the river; he was familiar with it; he had often heard them along the San Joaquin.

The day had been long, he had driven over 400 miles since leaving home, and he made another decision not to stay up late; instead, he prepared to turn in for the night. Before he left Madera, he had bought a truck camper shell, and then taken a piece of plywood and cut it to the exact dimensions of the Toyota's rear bed. He fastened it down with bolts, and on top of it he laid cheap beige carpeting he had found at a second-hand store. Now, he placed all his belongings on one side of the bed, and his sleeping bag on top of a roll-up mattress on the other. After making sure the doors were locked, he crawled in the back of the bed, closed the bed and shell doors, fell down on his bag, and was asleep within a few minutes. That first night, he never heard the desert all around him.

He awoke before the sun, when the first colors of dawn appeared above the mountains in the eastern sky. Looking through the shell window, he could see the light drifting across the landscape slowly like white lava, filling every canyon and gully with its glow. It reached the Toyota and crossed over it to the other side, where he could see the Colorado drifting sluggishly in the desert, not quite awake yet itself. He stretched, and in a few minutes was outside the vehicle, surveying the scenery around him. In September, it was cold in the desert morning; the thermometer he hung on the driver's side mirror read 47° F, although he knew that as soon as the sun came over the peaks it would heat up rapidly. He walked around for a few minutes, reliving the stiffness in his muscles and bones. Then he walked down to the river. It was still quiet, and the lights from Blythe on the other side still glowed in the semi-darkness. He could hear birds calling from downriver, and saw a sandpiper flying upstream, fighting the air as the fish fought the current. The river, vast and dirty, paraded past him and moved on. It added to the coolness of the air and caused him to zip up the thin jacket he was wearing. He watched the lights of Blythe turn off one by one in the dawn, and glanced around to see and hear the river and its creatures. Then he turned around and walked back to his campsite.

He puttered around with the Coleman stove for a few minutes, and finally got one of the burners lit. On it, he put an aluminum pot of water, and when it was hot, he poured it into a cup and added instant coffee. That, along with an apple, a small box of cereal, and a Danish roll, was his breakfast. He had never been big on breakfast; he'd always felt that he had too many other things to take care of in the morning. By the time he finished, the day promised to be a warm one, probably close to one hundred degrees. As the sun ascended, he could see more and more of the campground: the light brown sagebrush with occasional yellow or blue flowers sticking up, the light brown dust and sand, unbothered by rain for several months, the light brown hills sticking up in the background. He'd always heard that Arizona was a land of contrasts; now he surmised what the contrasts were: light brown and everything else. Looking back at the river, which was turning bluer in the sun, in defiance of the land, he decided to go hiking along it for the day. "I don't need to drive anywhere," he said to himself. "I'm in no hurry."

He intended to keep a journal of his trip, and in a spiral-bound notebook wrote, "September 9-drove from Madera to Blythe, camped at site on Arizona side near Ehrenberg. River nearby. Weather cloudless." Below that entry, he wrote, "September 10-up before dawn" and left the rest blank, to be filled in after dinner.

That morning, after putting away his journal, he sat down for a few minutes and lay back in his chair amid the scrub and the dust and the acacia trees. He closed his eyes for a minute and thought about what he might be doing otherwise now. He would be in his classroom, giving out an assignment on Puritan religious beliefs in early America. Or, he might be talking about Plato's dialogues about Socrates. Now, though, he was in a windblown camp on the California-Arizona border. He realized that he had played it safe for the past thirty years. He had to: he

12

had married and fathered two children and raised them to adulthood. But they were beyond him now, with their own lives and their own interests. In a strange way, Beatrice's death had given him a break-out message: time to let go and take more chances, time to find out about the world. He would do nothing foolhardy, but he now wanted to push himself and move beyond his little world. He thought of something he had heard years before: So many people never live a day; they spend their entire lives simply trying to keep from dying. He was now ready to start living again.

Eventually he got up from the chair and decided that if he was going to take a walk along the river he should do it soon. He put his camera and a bottle of water into his day pack, locked the Toyota, and commenced along the river. The trail was wide in some parts, almost undistinguishable in others, but he could follow it without any trouble. Every now and then, he stopped to photograph the desert flowers or the desert rocks or some other feature that appealed to him, but he never strayed far from the trail. At one point, he saw a raptor, a falcon, in the air, and watched it soar against the sky for several minutes until he lost it in the cliffs that lined the horizon. On another occasion, he spied a heron, wings outspread, float above the river water as if the currents were carrying it downstream along with the fish it was seeking. It, too, disappeared around a bend, and he was alone once more.

After a few miles, he turned back and retraced his steps to the campground and the Toyota. Everything was as it had been when he left, although he noticed that the other two campsites were deserted; the owners were apparently overnighters, they had pulled up and moved on, leaving him the only one in the place. That suited him fine; he wanted to be alone for a time. He realized that he was in fact very tired, not just from the initial drive, but from the preparation and the planning, and the summer school, and then the end of the school year, and most of all from the events dealing with his wife's death. He was utterly exhausted. Maybe it was not just the past seven or eight months, it was also the past three years, ever since Beatrice had become ill. It was all the doctor's visits, all the treatments, all the worrying while surgery was being performed, all the worrying while waiting for the inevitable test results, all the sleepless nights and ragged days. And of course, leading up to the final watch, the last few weeks, with Beatrice becoming weaker and weaker, the hospice watchers in the hallway, the almost constant flow of family and friends in and out of the house extending their wishes for a recovery but in reality saying goodbye. Finally Beatrice herself said goodbye, and could finally rest, but his rest had just begun and would be so for a long time.

He made a small lunch of a sandwich and an apple, and then crawled in the back of the camper and slept throughout the afternoon while the sky became hotter and the sun beat down on the beige and blue land.

He awoke and set up his stove and lantern for dinner. Afterwards, he cleaned up and relaxed in a folding chair and watched the sun recede and the stars turn in the sky. As it grew darker, he took his binoculars and looked up, trying to find a galaxy or a cluster; the night was embedded with stars, only there was so much that he soon lost track and gave up. As before, the glow from the town across the river spread across the sky, and he decided it was time for more rest and he took it. As he fell asleep, he could hear in the distance the howling of coyotes somewhere in the desert darkness.

In the early morning, he noticed paw prints around his campsite. They looked far too dog-like to be anything else, and he was sure that one or more coyotes had been around, probably smelling the food. "So, I had some visitors last night," he smiled to himself as he made breakfast. He made sure that before he left for the day, he'd have everything hidden and locked; no need tempting any animal to break into his vehicle and tear it up in search of food.

He finished, and was getting ready for the day's activity; this time, he planned to head inland, towards the cliffs a mile or two away, and see what secrets they held. As he left the site, he looked around and saw something move in the direction in which he was heading. Though his binoculars he could tell it was a coyote, maybe the same one that he had heard the previous evening. "I wonder what he wants," he thought as he walked off. The coyote looked over his way, and then moved quietly and deliberately, and soon disappeared behind some rocks. He made it to the base of the cliffs, but did not want to go beyond. For some reason, which he could not explain to himself, he felt that he should not trespass, as if they belonged to someone else and he was violating sacred ground if he did so. He scanned them for a time, watching the light and the shadow on them, then turned back and made his way down to the campground and the Toyota.

He returned in early afternoon, as he had done before, and again, took a nap, slowly reducing his sleep deficit. This time, he woke up much later, as the sun was setting, and he hurried to make a small dinner before it became too dark. By the time he was finished, it was dark night, and he was still tired, and crawled back into the Toyota, only this time, he slept lightly and could hear the sounds of the desert night, the call of an owl, the weird fluttery trill of nighthawks, the chirp of the cicadas. Above all, he again heard the howl of the coyote, and sometime

14

during the night, perhaps before dawn, he could hear an animal sniffing around his truck, trying to learn more of this visitor to its world.

When he emerged early the next morning he knew that the coyote, or a coyote, had been around his campsite. A new set of footprints was all around it, and not only that, the campground number post had a wet stain on it that ran to the ground. He remembered something he had read once and concluded, "Now he wants to tell me that I'm in his territory," so he decided to alter the territory. He washed the urine off and moved the truck about a hundred yards, to another camping space not far from the pit bathrooms. The smell was barely discernible and mostly downwind, but enough make an animal notice. He stayed around the truck all day, reading, and went to bed, and sure enough, did not have a visitor that night, although he could hear rustling and pawing in the sagebrush in the distance.

The next day, he had to go across the river and the border, into town to buy some groceries and other supplies. While he was there he talked to a man he had run into, an older man who, from his conversation, was a long-time native of the area, and mentioned the coyote among other things, and the man told him about the land.

"Yeah, you're at the campground across the river. Odd place. I lived there once for a while, until I got settled here. There's a coyote that's in that area, real curious, I assume it's still around, this was eight-ten years ago and they live a lot longer than that. It hangs around the camp trying to intimidate the people, thinks the area is his and his alone. I got to see him on occasion, he was never dangerous to me, but I never tried to outsmart him either. Interesting fellow. That might be the one you're seeing. The local Indian people talk about him as part of their legends. Their story is that he's the spirit of a member of their tribe, a chief, who lived here a hundred years ago or more. Knew about everything up and down the river, the cliffs, the sagebrush and trees, and still keeps watch over the area. You can believe that for what it's worth."

They talked about some other things and then parted ways. But he was intrigued by the man's story; he had thought of leaving the next day, but decided to stay a few more. He had dinner in town that evening, and when he returned to the campground at dusk, all was silent.

That night, though, he heard howls from up on the cliffs above the campground. They went on almost unceasingly, and he could not tell if it was one animal or several. They would start, then stop for a minute, then start up again, as if daring him to sleep. At one point, the sounds seemed to move from one place to another, and he thought he heard them to the east, then to the north, then to the south. But they always seemed to be the same distance from his vehicle. He tried his best to sleep, but, as dawn broke, he was bleary-eyed and wide awake.

He decided to get up. The morning was by now still, and the air had a distinct chill in it, for the first time since he had arrived. He wondered if this was the change of seasons, if this area did change seasons, or if it was due to the restlessness of the previous night. He was eating breakfast as the sun rose over the cliffs in the distance, and he resolved to climb to them, barriers or not, to find at least some trace of what had bothered him the night before.

He started up the path to the cliffs, almost directly into the morning sun, and its light spread warmth, almost a burning sensation over his face. The dust on the trail made scattered clouds around his ankles and legs, and boots slowly turned the color of dried mud. But he kept going. At times the trail was lost in shadows, but his feet, as if they had minds of their own, kept him on the path, steadily moving upwards. He noticed stickers and burrs that he was picking up as he moved along; they were on his socks and his pants. He brushed them off..

Far to the left, as he climbed, he noticed a form near the edge of the rocks that led to the cliffs. It stood watching him; he could only surmise that it was the coyote measuring his progress, and in a way keeping him going. He looked away for a second, and then looked back, and it was gone like a sprite into the rocks.

The day was advancing now, and he felt himself becoming warmer, sweat starting to stain his shirt. His heart was pounding, and he stopped to rest, and wondered if he should continue. But he thought to himself, "I'm in better shape than this," and made up his mind to reach the cliffs. At the same time, he saw the coyote again, this time near the top of the cliffs. It was staring down at him, as if challenging him to continue, communicating that he couldn't make it, couldn't come all the way. He accepted the challenge and kept climbing.

He stopped for a minute and wondered if this was all real. "Here, I am," he thought, "up here because of a story that I don't know if it's even true or not, told by some guy I never met before, who might be just having a fun time with a crazy outsider. Am I that big of a fool, or maybe I'm just paranoid?" He took a kerchief out of his pocket, brushed the dust off his face and hands and the sweat out of his eyes, looked around, and determined that, whatever his state, he would continue his climb. He collected himself, took a swig of water from his bottle, sized up his opponent, and moved on.

He came to the first rocks at the base of the cliffs. Here he was in shadow once more, and the chill struck him again. He moved slowly, as if afraid of slipping, and made his way over the dun-colored masses on the hillside. He was soon at the point where he had stopped a few days earlier, and once more felt the sense of un-belonging. But he also saw on the dusty ground between the rocks the doggish footprints of a coyote, and followed them into the sandstone monoliths. By now the sun was high in the sky, and he could see it through the crevices made by the tumbled rocks that made up the cliffs. As he passed a sharp edge, it caught his arm and the cut bled. He wiped it off with a tissue and otherwise ignored it. At another point, he had to grip a rock face with his hands, and the skin on a finger tore off and blood splattered onto the stone. He ignored that as well, and continued upward, into the sun.

Finally, he came to an open area and looked around. On three sides he was surrounded by rocks, but the fourth was an opening that led further up. He followed it. Every now and then he saw flowers growing out of the rocks, tenaciously clinging to the cliff sides, trying to grow and thrive despite all the barrenness. They were blue and violet and yellow. He did not know what they were, but he was careful not to damage them as he climbed up through the maze of stone. Advancing further, he could see more light, and finally came out into the open with rocks and piled stones all around him. He realized that there was no farther to climb and he was at the top of the cliffs.

He looked around. The sun was almost directly overhead, bearing down, and the sky was cloudless. To the west of him, he could see the campground and his car far below and in the distance. Only a bit further away was the Colorado River, a blue snake winding through the brown landscape of the desert. His eyes followed it downstream for several miles until it finally disappeared behind a bend. On the far side of the river was the town, spread out, dusty, and the green fields irrigated by the river, both appearing almost as mirages. He could see the highway moving out of the town and across the river, and he traced it from west to east it as it came across the land and then disappeared into the far horizon, a frail black ribbon on the vast landscape. "Beatrice would have liked this scene," he thought, and tears came to his eyes and he sat down for a minute to collect himself.

Then he heard a sound below him and looked down. There was the coyote, on a rock about a hundred feet away on the far side looking back at him. It said nothing, then turned around, jumped down into the rocks, and eventually disappeared. He never saw or heard it again.

He made his way back down to the campground, and that night, he sat in his folding chair and watched the sky darken and the stars appear and eventually the Milky Way came up over the cliffs. Once more, he took out his binoculars, turned towards the sky, and watched the stellar procession until he fell asleep in his chair. The next morning he woke refreshed, had breakfast, packed up the Toyota, and left.

17

October

He hesitated about calling, but then decided to go ahead and do it anyway. He wasn't even sure if it was the right phone number; it was over ten years old, and Dan, he knew, had moved, and could well have changed numbers by then. But he called as it was. The usual rings indicated that the number was still valid, then the voice mail clicked on: "You have reached the residence of Daniel Westerling. Please leave your name and phone number, and he will return your call as soon as possible. If this is a legal emergency, call his voice service at 346-6289. Thank you."

He disliked talking to voice recorders, but went ahead anyway. "Dan, this is Michael Lindstrom. I'm in town for a few days and just wanted to see if you were free for lunch or something. Give me a call when you can." He gave his phone number and hung up.

Dan, he thought, one of his best friends in college, second ranked student in the class, vice-president of the student body, president of the debate team, president of the pre-law association, president of a couple of other things, winner of the Dean's Medal at graduation, voted "Most likely to be President by age 50." While he began and settled into his teaching career, Dan spent two years at Oxford as a Fulbright Scholar, came back to the U.S., graduated first in his class from Boalt Law School, and as soon as he passed the bar exam, was hired by one of San Francisco's oldest and most prestigious law firms. Within a few years, he was one of the highest paid attorneys in the Bay Area, making a name for himself in local political circles and preparing to run for state office. Then he was recruited for a senior partnership at a law firm in Albuquerque, moved east, and ended contact with all but a few people. He was one of them.

Now, some fifteen years after he left California, Dan's life reminded him of his older brother, who left family and friends and essentially vanished. Dan had become kind of a mystery; he seemed to have simply dropped out of sight with few clues as to his whereabouts. His political career had apparently fizzled, and, as far as anyone knew, he was still practicing law in Albuquerque, although in what capacity he did not know, because neither Michael nor any of his other college friends had heard from him in several years. He wasn't even sure if Dan and his wife Michelle were still together; he surmised that something had happened from the irregular Christmas cards that happened to show up in December or sometimes January or February. If they had divorced, that was too bad; he liked Michelle, a soft-spoken young woman from Fort Bragg who had taught wildlife biology at San Francisco City

College before they moved. He remembered their wedding, in Golden Gate Park near the Japanese Garden. They had insisted on an outdoor ceremony; it was more "authentic," in Dan's words. Afterwards, he met Dan and Michelle on occasion when he and Beatrice had business in the Bay Area; they presented themselves as a happy couple, but he always knew that such impressions could be misleading. He also knew of Dan's ability to convince anyone of anything. Even at Davis, many were comparing Dan's charisma to John F. Kennedy and his speaking abilities to Franklin D. Roosevelt. If Dan had decided to enter marketing, he would have been the greatest salesman in the world.

He had lunch at a McDonald's, and was finishing up his burger when the iPhone rang. "Hello?"

"Mike, what a surprise. Where are you? What are you doing? It's been so long."

"Dan, I'm in town for a few days. Just wanted to see if maybe we could get together for lunch or dinner sometime."

"Sure, what are you doing tonight?"

"Nothing, really."

"Great. I know a place on Central Avenue near the University campus. It's called Il Vesuivo. You know where it is?"

"I can look it up and find it."

"Good. It's great to hear from you. Six. Is that okay?"

"That's fine. I'll see you then."

He drove down Central Avenue, a lengthy concourse of fast food places, gas stops, auto parts stores, and restaurants that surrounded the University of New Mexico campus. He found Il Vesuivo without any problem and pulled in. In the dark, it was garishly lit up, and he hoped that the food was as good as the sign implied it was. He parked the Toyota and walked inside. When the hostess asked him about a table, he replied, "I'm supposed to meet someone here. I'll check the bar." He wandered into the dark, conversation-thick room filled with people holding glasses or about to hold them. For a minute, he saw no one familiar. Then he heard a voice. "Hey, Mike, over here." The voice belonged to a tall overweight man at a table in the corner. He was already standing when Michael came over, and threw his arms around him with a forceful and grabbing bear hug.

"Mike, good to see you! You're looking great. Sit down and have a drink before we get something to eat. God, it's good to see you." He pulled out a chair and sat down opposite his old friend.

He could now see Dan up close, and even though the voice was the same, the physical appearance would have been almost impossible to

19

match. In college, Dan ran five miles every day, watched everything he ate, and told him a few weeks before graduation that he weighed the same as he did in high school. The man before him now was at least fifty pounds overweight, belly straining against his belt, jowls hanging from his face, massive double chin. But that wasn't what struck him. Dan was the same age as him, yet he looked twenty years older, lines running across his face and forehead, weathered reddened ears and nose, ragged liver-spotted hands, hair that was turning white. What happened to him, he thought; maybe this was why he rarely contacted me, or anyone else in our class.

He had no time to mull those thoughts, for Dan immediately launched into a dialogue that he tried to keep up with. "Mike, are you still teaching? You must not be since you're traveling right now. What's going on?"

"I took some time off and decided to travel the country. I've been on the road since early September. I'm on kind of a leave of absence, and promised my principal that I'd return next fall. But for now I'm just wandering."

"And your wife, what was her name…"

"Beatrice."

"Yea, Beatrice, is she still around, or did you two split?"

"Beatrice died, Dan. Cancer. That's sort of why I'm wandering around right now."

Dan paused for a second before starting up again. "Oh, that's too bad. I'm sorry to hear that. And you have…two…children? How are they doing right now?"

"Two girls, they're doing fine. One is in college, the other is an elementary school teacher."

"My two boys are doing great. William is at New Mexico State, wants to be a lawyer like his dad. John graduated last year and is working in Santa Fe. I've got a little girl, too. Katie, she's nine. She's going to grow up to be beautiful, I can tell. Sharp as a whip, too. She's going to go far, I know."

"And Michelle is fine?"

"Oh, Michelle. She and I broke up many moons ago. We just didn't get along, you know how it is. I caught her with another guy, and that was that. She lives in Los Cruces now and teaches at the state university, or as far as I know she does. Actually, Katie is by my second wife, Arlene; we were together for only a few years, and then she took off with some other guy, too. I've just had back luck with women. They can't keep their skirts down or their pants up. Katie lives with her mother here in Albuquerque, I see her twice a month, the judge screwed

20

me on child custody; I said I could take care of her, but Arlene's lawyer said I was unfit, the damned women's rights thing nowadays. Well, so much for that. I'm doing well otherwise, though, have my own practice now, doing a lot of drug and marijuana cases. With all this talk about legalization in the air, it's a whole new area of law, and I got in on it at the start. I sometimes have more work than I can keep up with. I'm thinking of hiring an associate soon, maybe two, to help out, the office gets real busy, with all the questions about the new drug laws, I'll have a gold mine for the next fifteen years..." His voice trailed off.

"I'm glad to hear that you're doing so well. And the Albuquerque life has suited you? Very different from the West Coast, you know."

"I can't complain. Life here is good. I sometimes get tickets to the Broncos games in Denver, or watch the Lobos play at the University. Used to go skiing almost every weekend at Sandia Peak, had season passes, but don't do that anymore, my back bothers me too much. I've made a lot of friends here, get around a good deal. Nope, can't complain at all."

Listening to Dan, he formed the notion that the man was leaving out some things about his life and experiences. But, then, Dan was always good at dissembling. He had heard him practicing for debates enough times in college. It was something he would work on later, if the time made itself important enough.

"Well," he said, "Let's go have dinner. I'm hungry."

"Oh, we can eat right here. I'll have the bar waitress bring us a couple of menus."

As they ate, Dan talked some more. "Yeah, I moved here to get away from the phoniness of the San Francisco legal scene. Too many people there want to impress you or flatter you. They all think they're the most important people in the world, and they pay lawyers huge fees to basically prostitute themselves to keep them thinking that way. I got tired of it after a few years. I told Michelle, 'Let's get out of here, go where people are more genuine,' and she agreed. When I moved here and started working, after a while I felt as if I had been conned. The other partners told me when I was hired that I'd be doing corporate issues and mergers, which was what I always wanted to get into. But within a few years, I was getting mostly real estate cases, which I've never had any real interest in. I told them that wasn't why I came here, and they told me 'Take it or leave it.' I decided to leave it, and moved to another firm. There I did tax law, not quite what I wanted, but still better than before. Finally, the firm dissolved after a bunch of lawsuits against a couple of the partners. So, I went into business for myself. Started my own one-man law office. This was, oh, seven-eight years ago. To be

21

honest, I'm not making as much as I did before, both Michelle and Arlene screwed me out of a lot of money, but I still do well. As I said, the new drug laws have brought in a lot of business, and that's my main area right now. I deal with real interesting people, to say the least."

As Dan recounted all this, Michael noticed that his old classmate kept ordering gin and tonics. By the time the meal was finished, he had counted at least four, as well as wine. Michael wondered if that were too much, but decided to say nothing.

They finished, and Dan insisted on paying the bill, winking, "I'll take it off my income tax." As they were getting up, Dan suddenly asked, "Where are you staying, Mike?"

"Oh, I'll just get a motel room somewhere. I'm going to be here only a couple of days."

"Nonsense, follow me, and you can stay at my place. I'll give you a key and you can come and go as you like. Whenever you need to leave, just go ahead. It's the least I can do for my old roomie."

"Well, I don't want to impose on you, or feel that you owe me anything."

"Not at all. I've got plenty of room. In fact, at times the house feels kind of lonely; the two boys see me when they can, and Katie is there only every other weekend. No problem at all."

"All right then. Thank you. It'll be nice to be in a regular house for a few days."

He followed Dan through the streets of Albuquerque to a residential area on the west side of the city. As they drove through the subdivision, he noticed that, while some houses and yards were neat and tidy, others were shabby. Michael thought, even with all the niceness, this seemed like an area that was beneath Dan's dignity and prestige, and again, thought about what had happened to him. Surely something more than two divorces to come to this.

Dan's house was a three bedroom, two bath suburban mainstay, with the clutter and mess not atypical for an older bachelor. Secondhand looking furniture, drink glasses littering the living room and kitchen, the light in the hallway burned out.

"Sorry, I haven't had the time to get a new one," Dan explained as he led him down the hall. "I'll try to get it done this weekend."

"Here," Dan stopped at a door, "Take this room. It's the boys' when they come to visit me." He stepped into a small bedroom with a single bed and clothes dresser, nothing more. It was plain, but better than a hotel room. "I'll get you a couple of towels. Sleep in if you want. I'll probably be gone by the time you get up in the morning. I'll leave a house key on the dining room table, so you can come and go as you want. Help yourself to anything in the kitchen. If I don't see you in the morning, I'll be home about six, and we'll go have dinner somewhere. Sound ok?"

"Yes, that's fine. Thank you, Dan. This is much appreciated."

"Not a problem at all. Good night and sleep well."

"You, too." The door closed, and a minute later he heard another open, then close, as well.

In the midst of sleep, he thought he dreamed, or dreamed he heard, the front door opening and closing in the middle of the night, but he dismissed it and slept on. New surroundings and circumstances, he assumed.

When he awoke and got cleaned up, Dan was gone, as he had said, and there was a key on the table. He pocketed it, and scrounged around for some breakfast. Dan apparently didn't rate breakfast high on his list of priorities. As there was only a few small cereal packs and some orange juice in the refrigerator, he decided to go out for breakfast, drive around and find a McDonald's or something in the area. In the meantime, he wandered around the main living area, looking at different artifacts. A small bookcase full of mostly cheap paperback novels, the dust on them indicating that they had not been read for some time; a cheap Wal-Mart variety clock on the wall; an old poster of The Eagles on the far wall; he and Dan and a bunch of other students had gone to an Eagles' concert while at Davis; a stereo system sitting on a cabinet; he did not open it, but assumed that it was full of records, tapes, and CDs. Next to it on the floor was a CSNY album that he remembered from college, and a 45 single; he picked it up, and read The Eagles' "Life in the Fast Lane." He put it back on the floor. Otherwise, the house had nondescript used furniture, the kind one might see at a Goodwill store.

Out of curiosity, he picked up a dirty glass from the coffee table. It had slightly smudged lipstick on it, and when he smelled it, the scent of alcohol was evident. Well, Dan was single, and if he dated women, that was his business. Then he noticed something else. The coffee table was old and scratched, which went along with the other furniture, but he could tell that there were very fine parallel lines here and there. He ran his hand over them; he wondered what could have made them. Then the phone rang from somewhere in the house. He let it ring, assuming that it was hooked up to an answering machine, and after five rings, it clicked on, and a voice came out, "Dan, this is Roger. I thought you were going to take care of my case today. Where are you, man? I need to get out of this rap and back on the streets like quick. If not, I'll have to find someone else, so get your ass on it." The machine went click again.

He looked at the lines again, and wondered.

He spent the day at the zoo, officially known as the ABQ BioPark Zoo. He had always liked zoos; he and Beatrice had made a habit of visiting them whenever possible. Maybe it was the appeal to nature, maybe it was the quieter surroundings, or maybe just the idea that animals, as long as they were fed and given comfortable enclosures, didn't say much. He remembered a student from many years before, who at first wanted to be a doctor, but then after a summer of doing volunteer work at a hospital, changed her mind and targeted veterinary medicine instead. When he asked her about it, she simply said, "Animals don't talk back." It was as good a reason as any.

While he was there, he had a sense of déjà vu at one point. In front of the bird aviary a fortyish woman with locks of prematurely graying hair spilling down below her bush hat, one of the keepers, was holding a Screech Owl on a gloved hand and explaining it to a crowd of onlookers. The little owl's head darted back and forth as if looking for danger while the woman talked about its habitat, food sources, and behavior. He stayed for a few minutes to listen, and thought that he had heard that voice somewhere before; soft-spoken, sing-songy, slightly drawn out. He looked at the woman's face, and it seemed familiar, too, but he knew that many people looked similar; he could not place it and eventually moved on to other exhibits.

When he returned to the house at six, Dan was not yet home, so he picked up an old Sports Illustrated magazine, sat in a stuffed chair, and waited. About 6:30, Dan showed up. "Sorry, pal, real busy today, the last client didn't get out of my office until almost six."

"That's okay, no need to apologize. You have a job to do. That's all."

"Ready for dinner? Let's just go down the street, I know a little corner place there. We can catch up on the old days there."

At dinner, they went over their college days and their classmates. One was a neurologist in Salt Lake City; another owned an electronics store in Sacramento; a third had quit his job, divorced his wife, moved to Oregon and lived on a commune farm. "Can you imagine it," said Dan, "A fifty year old hippie living in the woods. I always thought his brains were screwed up somewhere. You never know what'll happen to people. Do you have any idea of what happened to Janice Herrera? I had the hots for her, but I was too busy with school. I now realize that I should have just asked her out and had it done with. Boy, I would have liked to have gotten her into bed with me. She would have been a great fuck. So would have Lindsay Patterson. I can just imagine both of them now. Their boyfriends and husbands must have all kinds of fun with them."

Michael was a bit embarrassed; the Dan he had known in college would never have used that kind of language or talked about girls like that. When they were at Davis, his girlfriend was a quiet, studious, and very religious young woman named Shannon Williams, and he treated her like royalty. She even had him going to church and Bible study with her. After graduation, though, he didn't know what became of her, and wasn't aware of any more of Dan's romantic life until he received an invitation saying that he and Michelle were getting married.

As Dan talked, he observed the man, and noted that his nose was unusually red, as if he had long-running allergies, or some kind of chronic irritation. And Dan's fingers had scars on them as well.

The next morning, Dan was gone again by the time he awoke. And the phone rang again, leaving another message. This time, though, it was not a client. It was a woman, Dan's second ex-wife. "Dan, Katie has been waiting for you all week to come over and get her; I agreed to let you see her two weekends a month, and you're not even doing that; you missed last time, too. Dan, grow up and take care of your daughter, or we'll have to go back to court again." The receiver clicked off.

So Dan had lied to him about the girl. He wondered what else Dan might have lied to him about.

That day, he drove across town to visit the University of New Mexico. He wandered around for a while, then visited the anthropology and geology museums. He had not been on a campus since summer school, and, in a way, was heartened by the throngs of students moving from one class to another. It reminded him of what he would otherwise be doing, teaching in his classroom, preparing high school students for experiences like this. He realized suddenly, for the first time, that he missed teaching.

Dan had not indicated that they would meet for dinner that night, and so he just had dinner by himself on the way home from the university, and then went back to the house. Dan was not there, and left no note or indication when he would be home. Michael watched TV for a while, then went to bed.

The next two days he spent visiting around the area. One of them was to Sandia Peak, east of the city, where he took the tram to the mountaintop and looked down on hundreds of square miles of desert and mountain vistas. He reveled in the view, and knew that Beatrice would have liked it as well. She had never been to New Mexico, and would have basked in its stark natural beauty, the clearness of the deserts and

25

mesas, the purity of its environment. Beatrice was a romantic, a philosophical adventurer who delighted in discovery and wonder. The scenery, the mountain, the vast arid expanses and their treasures would have stirred her imagination. He felt sorry that she had never seen such a vista.

Another day he drove first to Santa Fe, and then up to Los Alamos, where he had never been before, simply to see where the atomic bomb had been built. In a sense, it was a disappointment; it reminded him of a college town, with the research facility the main campus, and all the supporting houses and businesses around it. He knew, nevertheless, that history had been made here, the world had changed because of this place. Lives had been indelibly altered because of what happened here.

Dan had told him previously that he was busy with court appearances and client meetings for the next few days, and would probably not be able to meet him for lunch or dinner. It was to be expected. Dan had his life and job, just as he would have if he were back in Madera. Still, for someone who had such high potential at one time, some of Dan's actions and discussions came as a shock to him. He did not see himself as a prude, but his parents had not raised him to be sloven and crude and vulgar, and especially so after he met Beatrice; she would not have expected him to be around such a person. If Dan had been the way he was now in college, he was not sure that they would have become roommates or even friends. He thought about Dan's current life as he drove back to Albuquerque in the darkness, and was even more thankful that he had met Beatrice and lived so long with her.

The next morning, he found a note on the kitchen table: "I'll be late again tonight, things are real busy, so just do whatever. I'll talk to you tomorrow." He looked at it for a minute, and decided to go out to breakfast again. He cleaned up and dressed, and was sitting in the living room reading a magazine, when he heard sounds coming from the back bedroom. He assumed that Dan had already left for work but found out, to his embarrassment a minute later. A young woman, completely naked, came down the hall into the living room, looking tousled and sleepy as if she had just awakened. She saw him with a look of astonishment and surprise, covered her crotch and breasts with her hands, and ran back towards the bedroom. He heard the door slam shut. A minute later, she called, "Who are you?"

"I'm not a prowler or a burglar, or a rapist, if that's what you're thinking," he replied. The door slowly opened and she came back out wearing an oversized bathrobe, Dan's, he assumed. He was still sitting in

26

the chair. She slowly approached him. "My name is Michael, I'm a friend of Dan's from college. He's letting me stay a few days while I visit the area. I didn't know that you were here." He figured that Dan had brought her home for the night. Looking more closely, he sized her up. She was slim, long black hair, golden-yellow skin, distinctive oriental features, she was probably Chinese or Japanese, he concluded, late 20s at the most, maybe not much older than his daughter Laura. "Why don't you sit down for a minute?"

"Oh, no, I have to go. I'm Stacy. Dan never told me that he had someone staying, otherwise we would have, well, not come here. I've got to get dressed and go. Excuse me." She turned to leave.

He said, "I'm leaving in a minute myself, so take your time." He got up. "I'll leave a note for Dan, and then get going."

Stacy disappeared into the back bedroom. He had the idea that she had been here before, but then, that was Dan's and her business; Dan was a bachelor, and he had no right to judge his personal life. Still, it unsettled him.

He was writing the note when he noticed two things. One was that there were more thin straight markings on the coffee table surface, along with the residue of white powder of some kind. The other thing he noticed was on a side table next to the sofa. It was a woman's wedding ring.

He spent the morning wandering around Albuquerque, and by noon found a beautiful park near the downtown area. It was a clear crisp October day, and he walked around it, admiring the trees and the shrubs, and watching the young mothers with their children, and the young lovers wandering hand in hand, and the older people conversing quietly, and the muffled sounds of traffic in the background, almost blocked out by the expansiveness.

As he meandered, he thought about everything he had seen and learned since he had arrived. Dan had left the Bay Area and a prestigious high paying position and essentially downgraded his career, handling street-level drug cases. He was twice divorced and sleeping with women half his age. He was neglecting his young daughter, and letting both his physical and mental self go south. While he was processing all this, his mind went over the people he had encountered in Albuquerque: Dan himself; the girl Stacy, who was apparently married to someone else; the voice of Roger, whom he assumed was a drug dealer; the other voice of his ex-wife Arlene; the sing-songy voiced woman with the owl at the zoo...the woman with the owl...He turned around and left the park, got into his truck, and drove to the Albuquerque BioPark Zoo.

27

After paying the entrance fee, he walked to the bird aviary in a controlled but excited way. Once there, he wandered through the structure, watching the various brightly colored inhabitants fly and flutter around him. He was hoping that she would be there, but was prepared to be disappointed if she was not. He was in luck. He saw her surrounded by people, this time with a macaw parrot in her hands. He waited at the edge of the group, listening to her melodic measured words as she talked about the brilliantly feathered bird that she held. She wore the standard uniform of zookeepers and docents everywhere: khaki pants, dark shirt, a khaki vest with a zoo patch on it, and a bush hat. This time, it was not just the voice that caught his notice, but her face as well. Project it all back twenty or so years, and…

He waited until questions had been asked and the remaining people had dispersed to other displays. Then he walked up to her. By now, he could read her nametag and was sure.

She looked at him keenly. "Yes, hello. Can I answer any questions about Sam, our macaw, or the other birds?"

He looked at her. "Yes, if I can ask you something. Are you Michelle Westerling?"

She looked at him in surprise, and her hand suddenly became unstable. The Macaw squawked, and instinctively she stroked its feathers to calm it down.

"You know," she said, "This sounds weird, but you resemble someone that I knew once. Can I ask you your name?"

"I'm Michael Lindstrom. I knew you and your husband from the Bay Area many years ago."

She almost forgot her poise, the Macaw, everything, and answered excitedly, "Yes, Michael! How are you? I never expected to see you. Do you live here in Albuquerque now? What are you doing here?"

"I'm traveling right now, I've taken some time off," he replied.

"Michael, this is wonderful, meeting you after so many years. Are you in a hurry?"

"No, not at all."

"I get off at four; can you wait around until then?"

"Certainly."

"Meet me outside the main entrance then. We can go and find somewhere to sit down and talk."

He spent the rest of the afternoon walking around visiting exhibits he had seen a few days before. At four, he was next to the entrance when she walked up. She was no longer wearing her zoo uniform, but jeans and a red sweatshirt and flats. "Here, come this way," she said. "We'll

28

go over to the park and find a seat and talk."

"I hope I'm not keeping you from anything. If so, just tell me."

"No, that's okay. I have to go somewhere later tonight, but I have some free time for now." They had been walking away from the zoo and into a park-like area with multitudes of trees and shrubs. "Here," she said, stopping a bench seat. "Sit down."

As they both took seats, he watched her intently. She was still slim and erect, but her face showed signs of distress and wear, and the grey in her hair was more extensive than he first realized. From the way she glanced at him, he was sure that she was doing the same thing.

Finally she said to him, "You're by yourself. I hope that doesn't mean that you and your wife, her name was Beatrice, wasn't it, have split up?"

"No, we didn't." He hesitated for a second, and then told her of Beatrice's illness and death, and his subsequent travel plans.

She grabbed his hand. "Oh, Michael, I'm so sorry to hear that. How terrible. I hope she died peacefully."

"Well, it wasn't easy, but it happened, and the rest of us survived, and I guess life goes on." He paused. "How are you doing, Michelle?"

She paused for a second also. "Oh, I'm doing well. I don't know if you're aware of it, but Dan and I are divorced. Have been for over twelve years now."

He looked at her and decided to reply directly. "To be honest, I'm staying at Dan's place. I called him when I got into town. He told me about it, or at least his side of it."

"He probably told you that I was awful and mean and greedy, and I was the cause of everything. The bastard. No, I don't mean that. In a way, I still love him, I just couldn't stand living with him anymore."

He looked at her and asked, "Michelle, what happened to Dan? The man I've seen over the last week or so is not anywhere near the person I once knew."

She sighed and took time to formulate an answer. Finally she said, "Michael, the best I can say is that he started believing in his own myth. He had never failed at anything. He was first in his class in high school, second or third at Davis, first in law school. I heard that over and over. He really thought he could do anything and do it well, and that anyone who thought otherwise was simply wrong. He let it all go to his head."

"When did all this begin? I didn't notice it at Davis. It must have all come afterwards. He was confident, I know, but there wasn't any of the arrogance or delusion or the physical degeneration that I see now."

She gave a long sigh again. "What I can say is that in San Francisco, things started to go bad. He was the golden boy, the hotshot lawyer with the best and biggest law firm in the city. He was invited to all kinds of parties and other social events. I was invited, too, but I got tired of them after a while. So he went anyway; he had it in his mind that they were for business. I'm not sure when but he got introduced to cocaine at one of them. Dan was making three hundred thousand a year by the time he was thirty, and he thought he was on top of the world. Basically, after a few years, he was a cocaine addict."

She paused, and then regained her breath. "It wasn't just that. It was the girls as well. They were like groupies following sports stars or politicians. Only in this case, it was up-and-coming glamor lawyers. They were at all the big social functions. Dan, of course, was always good with words. He started having affairs, one girl after another. He went through at least three or four, until everything came out one day. And that was because he was driving his latest fling to a hotel when he had an accident. Not only that, but she was the step-daughter of one of his firm's senior partners. As usual, I was the last to know. Anyway, the accident put Dan in the hospital, where his addiction was discovered, then in a rehab center. In the meantime, I found out that our savings accounts and other assets were almost depleted due to his hobbies. When he got out of rehab, the firm basically told him to quit or be fired. So he quit."

"And this was why you moved here?"

"Yes. No other San Francisco firm would hire him. He was toxic in the Bay Area. He was out of work for several months, and we lived on my pay from the college. So when he got an offer from a firm in Albuquerque, we talked it over and he took it, small as it was."

"He told me that he was a senior partner in Albuquerque."

"Michael, by now Dan was used to lying to make people believe anything he wanted them to. I decided to stay with him for that reason. We went to counseling, and he swore to me that it would never happen again, that we could start all over in a new environment, that everything would be better from then on."

She stopped talking for a while and sat silent. Around her the skies grew darker and a cold breeze began to blow. The leaves on the trees were rustling, protesting against the wind.

"He was never a senior partner. They gave him a second chance, and so did I. And for a while he did well, and I had hopes that things would in fact be better. It seemed like we had our lives back together, and I was happy with him and the boys. We had a nice house here and a cabin in the mountains where we'd go skiing in the winter and hiking in the summer. After a few years, I felt like we were a real family again."

"But it wasn't so?" he asked.

"No, it wasn't. And again, I was the last to find out. Dan was with a girl he had met at an after-hours get-together. She was at least ten-twelve years younger than him, and they were doing drugs together as well. He tried to explain it, but this time I just packed up the boys and whatever I could take and left. Got an apartment and a job and filed for divorce. And that was the end of our marriage."

"What do you do now? Dan told me that you're a professor somewhere."

"I wish. I work full time at the zoo and teach two Life Science classes at the junior college at night. It's enough to pay the bills and have a little bit left over. I really like the zoo. I've been there for about eight years now and love working with the animals, but it doesn't pay very much, and hopefully eventually I can move up to full time teaching, and have to work only one job. No, by the time the divorce settlement went through, there wasn't much. Dan had used up most of it. Even the cabin had to be sold to pay off some of the debts he ran up. After that, I was just happy to be out of it all. Dan was supposed to pay child support for the boys, but he never really has, and, rather than fight it, I just let it be. It's not worth it anymore."

"Not to bring up a sore subject, but Dan told me he has a daughter now as well as the boys."

Michelle nodded. "He remarried three years after we divorced, and Katie, the girl, was born five months later, so I assume that Arlene, that's his second wife, forced the marriage on him. I've met Arlene and Katie maybe two or three times. The marriage only lasted about three years. It wouldn't surprise me if Dan never left off his playing around with other women the whole time. The boys tell me that he's had a steady stream of girlfriends ever since then."

He thought about Stacy for a second, and decided not to bring her up. Let things be for now. Instead, he asked, "Are you doing okay now, Michelle? Is everything alright?"

"I'm okay. I live not too far from here, I have a fairly nice apartment. The boys are out of the house, but call all the time, and see me when they can. Well, William comes home from college for holidays and summers. I should be thankful; they're very protective of me."

"If I may ask, did you remarry, or are you seeing anyone?

"No, for a long time, I just focused on picking up the pieces and getting my life back into order to the point where I had some kind of stability and financial security. It's only been in the last two-three years that I've started going out and meeting people socially." She gave a wry smile. "Right now there's this doctor that I've been seeing. He's fifty-one, never been married, thought he would be a bachelor all his life.

Real nice person." She looked at him. "Are you doing okay?"

"Oh, I'm still here. In a sense, I'm picking up the pieces also. My two girls have been a big help; they were a major source of support in the last year of Beatrice's illness. The younger one, Danae, is living in my house now and hopefully taking care of everything while I'm gone, although I'm half expecting to find the place in ruins when I return. She's a college student, not a house owner or keeper." He grinned and she smiled with him. "Other than that, I'm okay. There's still a sense of numbness, as if this all isn't real and I'll wake up someday and find Beatrice still here."

She looked at her watch. "Michael, I'd love to stay and talk more, but I told Alan, that's the doctor, that I would meet him for dinner at seven. I hope you don't think I'm brushing you off. It just feels so good talking to you, I wish we could find some other time. How long are you going to stay in this area?"

"Probably not more than another day or two. I've been thinking that maybe I'm overstaying my welcome at Dan's. He was real enthusiastic at first, but now doesn't seem to have much time, like I'm getting in the way of his life."

She nodded, then searched around her pockets and found a piece of paper. "Here, let me give you my phone number and email address, if you change your mind about staying, or suddenly leave town." She handed the paper to him. He tore off a section of it, wrote down his information, and gave it to her.

He stood up to see her off. She looked him in the face and said, Michael, wherever you go and whatever you do, I wish you well. You lost someone dear to you, and I guess I did, too." She gave him a hug. "Strange, the people we run into out of the blue. Small world."

He replied sincerely, "Take care, Michelle. I hope to see you again. Maybe on my way back."

With that, she walked away, into the deepening evening sky.

In the note that morning he had told Dan to meet at the restaurant they had been at the first night, and to call him if anything were amiss. He heard nothing, so he assumed that everything was on. He thought about what Michelle had told him, and it bothered him that Dan could have fallen so far, maybe even further, since Michelle had not seen him in some time. Well, he felt sorry for his friend, but didn't know if he could help him, or if he even wanted help.

He waited at the restaurant for almost an hour, but Dan never showed, so he had dinner by himself, and then drove back to the house. He decided to leave in the morning, no matter what; he just didn't feel comfortable at the house anymore, and he had seen all that he wanted to in Albuquerque. He even thought that, considering what he now knew about Dan, he'd give Michelle some room, even though he wanted to talk to her more. It would have to be at another time.

When he pulled up to the curb in front of Dan's house, there was no car in the driveway, and a single light in the living room was on. He remembered there was a night light, and he figured that no one was home, so he opened the door and walked right in. He didn't expect to find what he did, although, given what he had learned over the last several days, he should have expected it. Dan and a girl, this time a fair-skinned brunette in her twenties, were on the sofa. They were both naked, and she was on top of him, straddling him at the waist. On the coffee table was a small packet of white powder, a razor blade, and some straws. It was obvious what they were doing, and it was also obvious what the powder was.

He didn't stare, he didn't gape or look surprised or offended. Instead, as they looked up at him, he said, "I'll just get my stuff, that's all." The girl jumped up and grabbed the sofa coverall blanket and covered herself in it, while Dan struggled to put on a pair of pants. He turned and walked down the hallway and into the bedroom. It took him only a minute or two to pack what few clothes he had and zip up his bag. When he came back out to the living room, Dan was dressed, and the girl, he assumed, was in the bathroom; he had briefly seen her run past the bedroom, and heard the door slam.

"Mike, I'm sorry about this. If I had known, I would have…" His voice faltered and for the first time he had known the man, he was speechless.

"Dan," he said, "You have a problem, and I don't think there's anything I can do about it. I can tell you to go into rehab and therapy, but I gather you've already done that, and it apparently didn't work. So, I don't know. You have my phone number, so if you ever need to talk to me, I'll be there. But from what I can see and from what I know, you need to convince yourself that you need help. I think I'll just get going for now."

"Really, I'm sorry, Mike. I mean it. I can get straightened out any time."

"Well, I hope so. I think it's time for me to go. It's been good seeing you, Dan, and I appreciate you letting me stay here. I hope things work out for you. Take care." And he extended his hand. Dan slowly brought his up to shake it, and then he turned around with his bag and walked out the door to the Toyota.

He got a room at the Super 8 just off the Interstate, turned off the iPhone, and had a troubled night's sleep. In the morning, after breakfast, when he turned the phone back on, he saw a message from Dan. He listened to it, decided to ignore it, packed up his truck, and continued on the highway out of Albuquerque.

November

He arrived in El Paso via Interstates 25 and 10 on a warm November day. It had been many years since he had visited this city; he remembered that the last time was when he had finished his second year of college, and, instead of finding a job for the summer, decided to go off and explore some of the country. He bought an old Chevrolet and filled it up with his camping equipment, and drove off on what he assumed would be a great adventure. It had sounded like a good idea, but he realized his mistake of traveling through the Southwest and the border regions during the summer, especially in July and August, when the temperature can reach as high as 125, and the nights rarely cool down below 100. After reaching El Paso on July 4 and reading 119° F on a bank thermometer, he turned north, to cooler lands. Now, though, in the fall, the weather was much more reasonable, and he decided to stop and spend at least several days in the area.

At first, he found a campground outside the city, but after a few days there, feeling the need for more civilized quarters, searched around and located a decent looking motel that charged only $35 a night. He moved in and estimated that he could stay there a week, and maybe a few days more until he would have to move on. For a while at least, he would have a clean bed to sleep in, a daily shower, a television to watch at night, and, with some frugality, two good meals a day.

He spent one day just driving around the city, poking into its cubbyholes and corners, learning where the parks were, what area had the best shopping, which sections seemed to be the safest. He spent another day at UTEP, the University of Texas at El Paso. He had heard about this school, and at least three of his former students had attended it. As he wandered around the campus and watched the students come and go, he was reminded of when he first met Beatrice, in the library at UC Davis. He was a third year undergraduate student then, majoring in history, and she, having already received her bachelor's degree at San Jose State, was in her first year of the graduate writing program. He remembered her vividly the first time they crossed the campus together, her graceful and slim, effortlessly walking, long hair flowing behind her like a dark tropical waterfall, light brownish skin accenting her strongly defined face and hands. In the student union café, they drank coffee and talked about their studies. She struck him as being far older and more mature than her stated age. Afterwards she would tell him that he was the one who seemed intelligent and wise beyond his years and beyond hers as well. They talked about history and literature and science and art and philosophy, and later about much more personal things. By the end

35

of the school year, they had made an unspoken commitment to each other, setting them on the trail that ended in the cemetery in Madera.

Once, several years before, he had visited Austin, and been on the main University of Texas campus there, which was a city unto itself, almost 60,000 students. UTEP was much smaller, but impressed him nevertheless with its starkly beautiful and clean campus. At times, he'd had students in his classes who were originally from Texas, and made a note in his journal that night to recommend UTEP to those who planned to return to the Lone Star State after they finished high school.

Another day, he crossed the border, and wandered around Ciudad Juarez, taking in the sights and sounds of the Mexican border city. He knew that, since 9-11, security at the borders was much tighter, and had brought his passport for such an eventuality. He also knew about the drug and gang problems, but neither presented themselves during his day on the other side of the Rio Grande, or the Rio Bravo, as the Mexicans called it. He wandered from one shop to another, scraped the rust off his Spanish, and enjoyed himself conversing with the storekeepers and officials that he met during his brief peregrination. Just to be sure that he didn't get lost, though, he re-crossed to the American side well before the sun went down, and felt so good about the day that he decided, on a whim, to have dinner at a small Mexican restaurant that he had noticed a few days earlier.

After some driving around, he found it. Outside, it looked like a shack that had seen better days, but he entered and found it to have a small cozy and clean dining room. Two of the walls were taken up with booths, while two rows of four tables each went down the center of the room. The walls were painted with scenes from rural Mexico: women in traditional outfits making tortillas, men bringing in their fish, children playing in the patio among chickens and dogs. Small white candles were lit, their light flickering off the walls, and vases of silk flowers garnished each table. A door to the right of the entrance led to the cantina, where he could hear a television set announcing a soccer game in Spanish. As he walked up to the front desk, a waitress in black pants and a white short-sleeve blouse came up with a smile. "Would you like to sit down?" she asked with only the very slightest Spanish accent.

"Yes, thank you."

"Is it just you, or are you waiting for others?"

"I'm the only one."

"Come this way, then."

She led him to a booth towards the rear of the room. He sat down and she took away the second paper placemat and the tableware, and gave him a menu with a list of specials.

36

"Would you like something to drink while you're deciding?" The initial banter reminded him of a thousand restaurants he had been to over the years. The faces and locations changed, only the questions did not. He wondered if every restaurant throughout the country used a standard book to train its service people.

"Water and a glass of white wine. Whatever your house wine is." She wrote down his request on a pad, and replied, "I'll be right back."

He studied the menu. The usual Mexican dishes. Burritos, chimichangas, chili verde, combinations with tacos, enchilladas, rellanos, rice, beans, the usual that could be seen on Mexican restaurant menus anywhere. He finally decided he'd splurge and ordered fajitas with rice and beans. He had not had it in several years, not since Beatrice became ill and was put on a strict diet. He unconsciously wanted to slip back into old habits.

The server brought his wine and he ordered. As she wrote on her pad, he noted her. Slim, an inch or two shorter than him, obviously Latina with smooth medium brownish skin, dark brown hair neatly pulled back in a bun, dark eyes that peered from out of a young-old face, thick eyebrows, and a furrowed forehead. Her forearms and hands were different, though, soft and fragile looking, like a child's on a woman's body, with the exception of two scars that ran down the right arm like cracks in a piece of fine delicate pottery. He estimated her age to be thirty-five, give or take a few years. She wore no makeup and no jewelry, although he surmised that may have been because of her job. The nametag on her breast pocket read "Luz."

Even though there were about twenty tables, only four of them, including his, were occupied, and she seemed to be the only server around. It was six p.m. and the place was not very busy. Maybe people here eat later, he thought.

The meal came with the usual chips and salsa, and then a salad. He nibbled on both while waiting for his meal. He took out his iPhone and scrolled through his messages and texts. He had forgotten to check his email for several days, and absently went through a huge list of messages, mostly ads. As he was finishing up, the woman brought him his food. He could hear and smell the sizzling fajita meat and vegetables long before they reached his table, and when they did, the server set them down in a cloud of steam. He thanked her and began.

The food was delicious, the best Mexican dish he had tasted in a long time, even in all the years that he and Beatrice went out to dinner. He understood that this dumpy little place was a rich treasure of cooking, and even before he finished, decided to return to it before he left the city.

When he finished, he looked up and realized that he was the only one in the place. He hadn't noticed that patrons at the other tables had departed. She came over and asked him if he wanted anything more. He shook his head, "No," and then told her, "This is maybe the best Mexican food I've ever had. It was wonderful."

"Thank you," she replied, and then he asked, "This looks real slow for an evening dinner rush. I hope it's not like this all the time."

"We get most of our business at lunch. If you came in here at noon, you might have to wait a while to get a table. We get a lot of takeout, too. Sometimes it's busy in the evening. Not tonight, though."

She laid the check down in front of him, and he was surprised at that as well. $14 for the fajitas and side food, salad, and glass of wine. Well, if the owners wanted to set the prices that low, it was their prerogative. She was a very good waitress, he decided, and put down a twenty next to the bill before getting up. At the front desk, he stopped and told her, "Thank you for a very good meal."

"Thank you for coming. Come back again." Her dark young-old eyes followed him as he started to turn away.

"I may do that." And he left.

Three nights later, he decided to go back to the Mexican restaurant. He arrived a bit later than the first time, around seven, but this time, the dining room was more crowded, with only three tables open. An essence of chatter and Mexican food greeted him as he walked up to the front desk. Luz was standing there, examining a seating chart. She looked up and the eyes stared into his face. "Hello. So you did come back." She remembered him, to his surprise. He had assumed that she had so many repeat customers that she probably couldn't keep track of all of them. "Would you like a seat, or is this takeout?"

"A seat, please. Whatever is open. I guess I don't have the choices I had last time."

"Yes, tonight is busy." She took him to another booth, this one two down from where he had sat the previous time. She asked him the same questions, took his order, and then went off to check on her other tables.

When she came with his main course, this time chili verde, she asked, "You're not from this area, are you?"

"I'm from California, more specifically the Central Valley, a town north of Fresno called Madera."

"And what brings you to El Paso?"

"I'm a traveler, a wanderer, if I want to stretch it, a pilgrim maybe."

"This may sound stupid, but I thought pilgrims were the people who came over on the Mayflower and had the first Thanksgiving with the Indians. At least that's the way I learned it in school. "

"Well," he replied, "I'm not quite that old," and they both smiled. "No, a pilgrim is someone who goes on a journey for religious or spiritual reasons."

"You sound like a schoolteacher."

"I am."

She started to say something more, then looked around, said, "Excuse me," and suddenly left. A minute later he saw her coming out of the kitchen door with a tray of food and carrying it to a table of four on the other side of the room. He decided to eat. Every once in a while he looked up from his food and saw her serving a dessert, presenting a check, or running into the bar. All the time, he noticed the dining room was thinning out, and by the time he finished, only two other tables beside his own remained. The background noise was now quiet whispers from across the room.

She came back up to him, "Is everything alright?"

"Yes, very much so."

"Is there anything else I can get for you?"

"No, that's fine. I just noticed that you got busy for a while."

"I didn't mean to run away in the middle of a conversation, but I had dinners coming up. We get our food orders from a pager in the kitchen." She showed the device on her belt.

"That's okay. I would have done the same. Don't worry about it."

By this time it was approaching eight-thirty, and the other two tables got up to leave. She went to the front and took their payment. When she was finished, she came back with his check and put it on the table. She looked at him intently, and said, "So you're traveling."

"I decided to get away for a while and see what the country is all about. I know that sounds kind of farfetched and romantic, but it is what it is. That's all."

"I noticed that you're wearing a wedding ring."

He looked down at it. He had been wearing it for so long that it had simply become a part of him, like his arm or his stomach or heart. He hadn't really thought of taking it off after Beatrice died. It was the first time since Beatrice's death that he realized he still had it on.

"Excuse me for being so direct. It means that your wife left you and you don't want to admit it, or you've left her, but still want to act married, or maybe..."

"I'm still married but want to be with someone else?"

"Well, yes," she finished.

"Well, actually, it's none of those at all. My wife died eight months ago from cancer."

She suddenly put her hand over her mouth in surprise. "Oh, I'm so sorry, I never meant to imply, oh, I'm so stupid, oh, please forgive me…"

"No harm done. You know, I sometimes still think that I'm married. I imagine it takes a while to get over that."

She looked around; the dining room was empty except for the two of them; noises could be heard coming from the kitchen and also the cantina. The sun had gone down, and the only light came from the candles on the tables and the illumination through the kitchen doors.

She reeled back, and replied softly, "Please don't tell anyone here what I said, it just kind of came out, I didn't know and simply concluded…"

"Don't worry about it. I probably would have thought the same thing if I were in your position. Actually, it's kind of nice to tell that to someone who's not in the family or a close friend; I don't think I've done that up to now. I guess I have to start getting used to it."

I owe you an apology. I owe you something. I don't even know your name."

"Lindstrom, Michael Lindstrom."

"I'm Lucia Villanueva. I've been called Luz ever since I was a child." She lowered her voice a bit more. "There's a twenty-four hour Denny's about four blocks down from here." He nodded; he had passed it on the way to the restaurant. "I get off at ten. Meet me there a little bit after. I owe you coffee and pie and an apology."

"You don't need to do that. "She looked at him with a Yes-I-Do expression. "All right, I'll be there about ten." He paid his check, left another large tip, and left.

He arrived at the Denny's at ten, was seated, told the waiter that he was expecting someone, and ordered coffee. At about ten after, she came in, still wearing her uniform and an old but clean blue sweater. He stood up as she came to the table, pulled out a chair for her, and motioned her to sit down. He immediately noticed that she was surprised by this.

She immediately launched into a fusillade of apologies. "I'm so sorry, I never thought about that, I can't imagine what you were going through, I feel like an idiot, I want to go home and shoot myself."

He laughed. "Don't do that. The world would lose a very pretty and, from what I've seen at the restaurant, a hard working person."

She started. "You really mean that?"

"Yes, I do. I wouldn't have said so if I didn't mean it. If you ever run into my students, they'll tell you when I say something, it's to be taken seriously."

"What do you teach, Mr. Lindstrom?"

"Call me Michael, and I teach history, high school level. If I were back home in my classroom right now, we'd be going over the years leading up to the Civil War."

She looked away for a minute, then came back to him. "When I was young, I looked up to schoolteachers. I often thought of becoming one, but things just didn't seem to turn out that way."

"If I may ask, Luz, how did things turn out?"

"Up until a few years ago, I was just making one bad decision after another. That was my life for a long time. I hope that now I'm on the right track, but I sometimes think it's too late."

He looked at her intently and with sympathy. "Again, if I may ask, what were your bad choices?"

She stared at him as if expecting immediate answers. "If you'll tell me your story, I'll tell you mine."

He started in, "There's not a lot to tell. Three years ago, I was a fairly successful high school teacher, doing well. My wife, her name was Beatrice, was a part time English teacher at a junior college, and also an author of novels and short stories. We had two daughters. One day, she went in for a routine mammogram. When she got the results, they said that the doctor wanted to do it over, and also come back for a follow-up breast exam. That's when they found a lump. She first went on chemo, then had surgery, then chemo again. They thought they had gotten it all out, but apparently not. A year later, it was back and starting to spread. Last December, right after Christmas, she made a decision to go off chemo and all other treatments, and let things take their course. She died on March 1, and we buried her six days later. That's about all there is."

She looked at him with sorrow and sympathy. "It must hurt you to have to tell that."

"No, not really. Those are just the historical facts of the story. I'm a historian, so I guess I tell things that way. Maybe someday it'll go deeper, and then it'll start to really hurt. I'm not sure when that'll be. I guess I haven't come to it yet."

"Do you have a picture of your wife? I'd like to see her."

He took out his iPhone and scrolled through the images stored on it, until he found the ones he wanted. He showed her a picture of Beatrice before she had the disease, cheerful, smiling; and then another, with her head in a turban to hide the hair loss from chemo. She was thin, then from the hair and weight loss, but still smiling, still trying to be

41

cheerful, even though her fate was taking over her.

"Here's our daughters. This one is of Laura." He flipped through the images. "And this is Danae. Which reminds me, I have to send them an email before I go to bed tonight. When I left, I promised them I'd check in every once in a while."

She smiled. "They're acting like your wife now, keeping tabs on you. How old are they?"

"Laura is twenty-five and an elementary school teacher. She got married about a year ago. Danae is twenty-one and a third year student at UC Merced." He saw a puzzled look. "UC means University of California, Merced is one of its campuses, kind of like UTEP-University of Texas El Paso. Anyway, when I left, she was planning to major in psychology, but it may be different by the time I get back. They're both good kids."

"And you are how old?"

"Fifty-two."

"What age was your wife when she died?"

"Fifty-four."

She looked at him in surprise. "So she was two years older than you. Did that bother you?"

"Not at all."

"That usually doesn't happen in Hispanic culture. In most cases, the man is older than the woman. Sometimes by several years."

"I've heard that. The school I teach at is about 70% Hispanic. The kids tell me about their parents and their home lives. Some are good, but unfortunately, others aren't."

"Mine is one of those that wasn't."

"Why, what happened?"

"The usual young person thing, making bad choices, only, in my case, making more bad choices on top of other bad choices. My parents came from Mexico. My mother got a high school diploma, but my father never went beyond ninth grade. He worked hard, though. Did everything. Field worker, truck driver, busboy, auto mechanic, he and my mother worked day in and day out to make sure we got ahead. And I was doing well up to about seventh grade. Then he died when I was thirteen. Killed by a hit-and-run driver. We didn't have much, my mother was gone working all the time, and I started skipping school and running around. Got boy crazy. You probably have girls in your school like that." He nodded. "Anyway, when I was fifteen, I met this guy who I thought was so wonderful. One thing led to another, and I was pregnant by my sixteenth birthday. As soon as he found out he was going to be a father, he disappeared. I never saw him again. Anyway, I dropped out of school, had the baby, a girl that I named Guadalupe, and she and I lived with my mother, my sister, and brother. I took care of Guadalupe and worked whatever jobs I could: restaurants, field work, things like that. At eighteen, I met another guy, he was a lot nicer and caring and had a lot of money and, and, when I was nineteen, we got married. I thought things were going to be okay. Then I learned how he made his living. He was a big drug dealer. I was scared of him and scared of what might happen to him. I got pregnant, and then had a miscarriage. I was pregnant again when he was found dead in an alley about five miles from here. Gunned down, gang execution style, according to the police. I was a widow with two young daughters at age 21."

"You've had it hard."

"Well, I don't know why I'm telling you this. I moved back in with my mother, and about two years later met another guy. Again, he seemed to be real friendly and caring at first, and, well, I got married again at twenty-four. Once we were married, though, he turned into a real asshole, there's no other word for it. Always suspicious, always accusing me of being with other guys. When he would go out somewhere, I was told not to leave the apartment; if I did and he found out, he'd beat me. One time he came at me with a knife. That's how I got these scars," and she held up her arm. "I was pregnant twice more, and both ended in miscarriages, probably because of the beatings. My mother had gone back to Mexico to take care of her parents, so I didn't have anywhere to go. The final thing was when he tried to rape Guadalupe; she was thirteen at the time and I had gone food shopping. She fought him off and cut him with her fingernails, and she was able to get out of the apartment. She waited outside for me until I got home and told me about it. When I confronted him, he yelled that she was lying and beat me for believing her, and finally I wanted no more of him. When he left for work, I packed up everything I could in a suitcase and left. We, myself and Guadalupe and Esperanza, spent the first night on the streets; we had nowhere to go. The next morning, I saw a police car and stopped it and told the officer what happened to us. He took us to a police station, and I told my story to the people there. They called a shelter home and someone came and took us to it. I heard later that the police arrested my husband. Some people he knew posted bail for him, and as soon as he was out, he disappeared. No one knows where he went or where he is. I think he went across the border to Mexico to live in one of those little towns in the mountains. Anyway, the people at the shelter helped me find a job and another place to live, and eventually I got a divorce. Since then, I've been working and staying away from men in general."

43

While Luz was talking, he thought of his sister. She too had made poor decisions at a young age involving men, and the consequences had haunted her ever since as well. He shook his head and came back to the present as Luz finished up her story "... For a long time I didn't want to have anything to do with men. No offense intended."

"Not all men are like the ones you had. There's a lot of good guys out there, believe it or not. I like to think that I'm one of them."

"I think you are, too. That's probably why I'm telling you this."

"What happened to your daughters? Where are they now?"

"Guadalupe stayed in school, and graduated last year. She went into the Air Force, and got accepted into nurses' school. That's where she is now. Esperanza is fifteen. She's a freshman in high school. I'm trying to make sure she doesn't make the same mistakes I did. Hopefully, she won't."

"What about yourself, Luz? Do you want to go further than working in a restaurant for the rest of your life?"

She sighed and was silent for a minute, then spoke slowly. "Once I really thought I could be a schoolteacher. I liked school and a couple of my teachers. Right now, though, I just want to make sure my girls do well and have it better than I did."

He looked at her closely. "Ever thought of going to college?"

She stared in puzzlement. "But I don't even have a high school diploma."

"If Texas is like California, you don't need a diploma to go to a junior college. All you have to be is eighteen. I assume that El Paso has a junior college. Here, I'll look it up."

He pulled out the iPhone and tapped in search engine addresses and clicked on links, and a minute later held it up for her to see. "Here it is. Why don't you go over and see about enrolling. It's too late for the fall semester, but you can probably start in January. If you want me to, I'll take you over there."

She looked at him with doubt and suspicion. "Why are you doing this for me?"

He sat back and stared thoughtfully at her. "Maybe it's because, as you said, I'm probably a good person. Also, as a teacher, I help young people achieve their goals. You once had a goal to be a teacher. I think it's still there, and you should go for it. It doesn't matter how old you are. At the high school, we've had people who didn't start their teaching careers until they were forty or older." He looked at his watch; it was almost midnight. "I'm probably taking up your time. Listen, here's my phone number and email address. I'm going to be here for at least a few more days. If you think about it and change your mind, contact me and

44

I'll meet you and we'll go over to the junior college together so you can get information and enroll if you really want to. I get the idea that you deserve more than waiting tables in a restaurant for the rest of your life."

He spent the next couple of days exploring the area. One day, he hiked in Guadalupe Mountains National Park, a beautiful range of peaks jutting up from the West Texas plains. And since Carlsbad Caverns was not far away, he stayed the night in a cheap campground, and visited them the next day. On another, he backtracked a bit and drove over to White Sands National Monument near Alamogordo, in New Mexico. The vast tracts of white grains, like mountains of gleaming virgin salt, fascinated him, and he wandered through their surreal landscapes before, regretfully, working his way back to El Paso.

Shortly before he crossed the El Paso city line, he received a phone call. He heard the ring, but didn't want to answer it while driving. Later, at the motel room, he listened to the voice mail message; it was Luz: "Mr. Lindstrom, I've thought a lot the last few days about what you said about going to school. I've been out for a long time, but I want to try it. Even my daughter says I should, but I don't know what to expect. I'd like to go over to the campus, but can you come with me as a kind of support? Would tomorrow be okay? Call me back." He did call her back and said that, yes, he would go over to the junior college with her. Ten o'clock the next day.

He met her in the parking lot of a shopping center a few miles from his motel. She was wearing off-work clothes: worn blue jeans, burgundy pullover sweater, tennis shoes. He had never seen what she drove, but she pulled up in an old dark grey Ford Focus. She greeted him with a hello and a smile; her hair was down, and came below her shoulders in wavy patterns. He liked the fact that she did not wear makeup.

"Here," he said, leading her over to the Toyota. "I got you into this, I'll drive," and opened the passenger door for her.

In time, they found El Paso Junior College, parked in the visitor's lot, put quarters into the meter, and noted the time. If they went over, he could run out and feed more to the maw of the parking machine. A message board next to the lot held a map of the campus; they found the admissions office and walked towards it.

The process went much the way he figured it would. The secretary at the admissions office desk reassured her that she could attend, and took her to a counselor, who explained the procedures and the GED program to her. After that, another assistant took her to the computer lab, turned on a machine, and brought up the application website. Forty

45

minutes later, Luz was enrolled at the junior college, starting with the spring semester in January. When she asked how much it would cost, the reply was that if she brought in her tax forms showing her income, the fees could probably be waived.

When it was all finished, she looked at him and smiled a smile that said Thank You, but much more as well.

They left the admissions building; he suggested that they find the bookstore so she would know where and how to buy her books. They found it and wandered around for a time. Then he looked at his watch; it was almost one o clock.

"Would you like to get some lunch somewhere?"

"Is it that time already? I have to be at work at four."

"We'll go someplace real quick, and get you back to your car. How about just eat in the food court here? Most colleges have pretty good food courts now, lots of different kinds of selections. Not like the cafeterias when you and I went to school."

They did, and both had good meals. He drove her back to her car at the parking lot and let her out.

As they were walking to her car, she said, "Michael, I can't thank you enough. I just feel like something good just happened to me, for the first time in a long time."

He said, "Thank you also, and you're welcome. You're not only pretty, but I think you're bright, always have been, and you need to go with it. You'll do well, I'm sure."

They arrived at her car, and she opened the door. "How much longer will you be here in El Paso? Are there other places you have to go?"

"I have a cousin who lives in St. Louis. When I left California, I told her that I'd be there for Christmas. That's the only real deadline I have right now."

She was very shy and quiet. "I have to work the next couple of days. Can I call you in maybe three days and we can meet somewhere? I know that sounds very forward, but I'd like to see you again before you leave. You've done me so much good."

He was reflective for a second and his emotions were twisting and tumbling. Then he replied, "Yes, I'd like that. I'd like to see you again, even if it's just at the restaurant."

She smiled, "No, not at the restaurant, somewhere else. I'll call you for sure. And again, thank you so much." And before she slipped into the driver's seat, she suddenly reached out and kissed him on the cheek, and then got into the car, waved goodbye, and drove away.

She talked to him three nights later, as she promised. "Michael, my work schedule has changed, and I have to go in tomorrow night. But I'd like to take you somewhere tomorrow, and then maybe we can go to lunch. Does that sound all right?"

"Yes, that sounds good, I'd like that."

"I'll meet you in the same place, again at ten am. Oh, bring your camera, if you have one"

"I do, and I'll be there."

She met him in the parking lot, and they drove away in her car; she insisted. They traveled southeast for several miles, then she turned off on a road outside of town. The road led to a park on the Rio Grande. She stopped the car and they got out.

"From what you've said, you seem to like to be in the outdoors. I thought of this place. I remember coming here sometimes with my parents and brother and sister when I was young. I had to look it up on the map last night because I really didn't remember how to get to it. I hope you like it."

He took it all in, the seemingly endless cottonwood trees, the river, the green grass he had seen so little of in the city. A soft cool breeze was blowing and the sky overhead reflected blue diamonds. They walked along the trees, and he took pictures from various angles. "You're right, this really is a beautiful place." He looked across the river to the far side. "I assume that's Mexico over there."

"Yes, it is. You know, it's strange that I've lived in El Paso all my life and I speak Spanish, but it's been years since I've been across the border. When I was young, though, we used to go to Mexico a lot to visit my grandparents and aunts and uncles and cousins."

They walked along the river for another hour. She talked more about her family, her older sister who left El Paso at eighteen and now worked for a graphics design company in Austin, and her younger brother, who joined the Marines out of high school, served tours in Afghanistan and Iraq, and was currently a sergeant stationed at the U.S. Embassy in Buenos Aires. "They got out and have done well, and I'm the one who stayed. Maybe I should have left, too."

"Trite as it may sound, I believe that everything happens for a reason. There's a reason you stayed here, despite all your difficulties. It sounds like you have two lovely children, and you can see your mother, I don't know what else. Look at it like that. I know I sound like an optimist, but that's just the way I am." He paused for a second. "Let me change the subject. Go stand by the tree and I'll take your picture."

She laughed and did as he asked. Afterwards, they walked back to the car. She asked about what Beatrice was like, and he told her, as much as he could, what he could find to say. He found that he could talk about his dead wife, the words came out less painfully than he might have previously thought, and he was glad for it. "Maybe I should have gone into therapy after she died, and 'get all my feelings out,' as they say, but I felt that I just wasn't ready for that either. Maybe it has to come out little by little until I get used to it. Anyway, I do have a lot of good memories about Beatrice. She was very good to me, we rarely argued, and disagreements didn't come too often. It was like we understood each other from the beginning."

Back in the city, she took him to a sandwich shop that she knew and sometime frequented. It was like the restaurant, dilapidated on the outside, but serving good food on the inside. They talked some more about their families and their lives, until she realized, "It's almost three. I have to go. I have to be at work at four."

On the way to his car, she was silent, as if she were thinking deeply of something. When they arrived and he started to get out, she turned to him and asked quietly, "Michael, I would like to ask you, and you don't have to if you don't want; I get off at nine. Would you like me to come over to your room after work for a while?" She looked at him in silence, wondering what his answer would be.

He paused for a minute and thought it over. Then he asked, "What about your daughter?"

"She's spending the night with my mother. Whenever I work late, after school she goes over to her place."

He nodded, and thought again. As with the previous invitation, his mind was in turmoil. Then he slowly said, "Yes, all right." And she nodded, too.

They both got out of the car, and she came over to him and hugged him. Then she suddenly asked, "Oh, what is your room number? I don't want to be knocking on the wrong door."

He laughed. "Wouldn't that be a surprise to someone, especially if his significant other is in the room? It's 117."

"About nine tonight, then?"

"Yes."

He had just completed writing an email letter to a colleague at the high school when he heard a knock on the door. He answered it, and she was standing there, still in her work uniform, slightly nervous, he could tell. He was nervous too. Ever since they separated that afternoon, he had been debating the decision in his mind, going back and forth, wondering whether he had made the right choice or not, wondering if he was betraying Beatrice by saying "Yes." Wondering if he was betraying Luz and himself as well. Finally, he instinctively decided to let things take their course and accept the consequences, whatever they would be.

"Come in, come in."

She entered and he could tell that she was looking over the room. It was small but clean and cozy: one bed neatly made up, a desk, clothes drawers, an open closet, and a door that led to the bathroom. She looked at him; he held up his arms and hands, and replied, "This is home for now, such as it is."

She smiled. "It's really quite nice. Much better than I expected. I assumed that most men's rooms were real junkyards, unless you've spent the last hour cleaning just to impress me."

"No, I've always kept it more or less like this. My wife always told me I was a neatness freak; I would keep things cleaner than her most of the time. Would you like something to eat or drink? I'm afraid I don't have much except some snacks and soda."

"No thank you. Actually, I'd like to do something that probably sounds out of the way and absurd to you. Do you mind if I took a shower? Esperanza says that when I come home from work, I smell like fajitas and refried beans, and, to be honest, sometimes I feel like that."

"Go ahead. Let me make sure there's a clean towel and washcloth and soap. He disappeared into the bathroom and came out a minute later. "All yours."

She asked, "Do you have something I can wear after I get out of the shower? I don't want to have to put dirty clothes back on."

He went to his bag. "Here, take one of my dress shirts. I don't know why I brought them, but I did, and they might as well be used."

It was her turn to vanish into the bathroom. After a few minutes, he could hear the water running, and turned to tidy up what little was left to be done. When the door reopened, he was sitting on the bed, reading a magazine.

She came out dressed in his shirt, and, as far as he knew, nothing else. She was carrying her clothes, black shoes on the bottom, white lace bra on the top, and put them down on the clothes chest. She came over to the bed and sat on it next to him. "Thank you for letting me do that. I feel much better, and cleaner. You wouldn't want me all smelly."

He looked over at her, put his arm around her, and pulled her close to him. "Actually, I'm glad you're here. I doubt if I would have suggested this myself." Then he reached over and took a small brown bag out of the night stand. "After you left, I went to a drugstore and got something in the event that we needed it."

She looked at him with admiration. "We don't. After my third miscarriage, I went to a woman's health clinic and made sure I wouldn't become pregnant again. It's not going to happen. And don't worry; I don't have any STDs. I made sure of that a long time ago as well."

"Neither do I."

He leaned over and kissed her, and she kissed back hard and long. He ran his hand over the shirt and down the side of her body and felt the curves and nothing over them. A minute later, the shirt was unbuttoned and on the floor, and she was what he thought she was, and both gave into passion and their world became only themselves.

Later, they lay on the bed resting, she was up against him, the brownness of her skin contrasting with the paleness of his. Her head was on his shoulder and she was stroking his chest. "Michael," she said softly, "Up to now, I always felt that I was being used by a man, by my husbands. But I didn't feel that with you. You're very caring and I appreciate it."

He looked at her, "I didn't know how I was going to react. I just did what I did."

"Is this the first time you've been with a woman since your wife's death?"

"It's the first time I've been with any other woman since my wife and I started dating, and that was over thirty years ago. I'm afraid I'm just a terminal romantic."

She laughed. "I like that. You're faithful. I wish my husbands had been."

"I guess it was just the way I was raised. My parents were married over fifty years, and as far as I know, neither of them cheated on each other. I always thought that that is what marriage was supposed to be like."

She glanced at his wedding ring. "Do you feel like you just cheated on your wife right now?"

He thought for a minute. "Well, yes, I do. I kind of debated that to myself before you came."

"As long as I brought it up, I'll say that this is the first time I've been in bed with a man since I left my second husband."

"I never wanted to ask. You're very attractive and personable. I figured you had gone out with at least a few other men before now."

"No. Guys come into the restaurant who want to take me out; it's happened a lot. But I could see that most of them were like my husbands, especially the second, and I just don't want to get involved with them. A lot of them are married, too. Maybe I just don't trust men anymore, I've been stabbed too much by them, so I've just stayed away."

"Is that why you asked about my wedding ring that night at the restaurant?"

"Yes. They're cheating on their wives, and I don't like that. I consider them far lower than those who are single."

"But you've trusted me? Why?"

"Somehow I could tell you were different. By the way you talked and acted. Maybe you're more educated, more refined, you seemed more caring. Anyway, after you first came in, I was hoping you'd come back, even though I really didn't know you at all. But I'm glad you did come back."

"I'm glad I did, too." And he pulled her close, and she kissed him again, and they began all over.

In the middle of the night, she heard noises and awoke. She was laying naked on the bed, covers off, and he was next to her, making half-recognizable sounds, moaning and sobbing. She could hear him saying, "Beatrice, Beatrice...I'm sorry..." in a strangled voice. "Michael," she whispered, "Rest, quiet and rest..." but he continued. "Michael," she said, and took his head in her hands and moved him on top of her so that his head was between her breasts and he could hear her heartbeat, and she stroked his hair. "Michael, rest..." She did this same thing when her daughters were restless or had nightmares, especially Guadalupe after the rape attempt, letting them listen to her nurturing heart until they fell back to sleep in peace, and now he did the same, and they both rested.

He half awoke, drowsy, and she was on the side of the bed with her clothes next to her, starting to get dressed. "Michael, go back to sleep," she said quietly. A minute later, she went to use the bathroom, and then came back and finished dressing. She went to sit by him on the bed, "Michael," she said, "I'd like to stay, but I have to go."

"What time is it?" he asked.

"About five."

Now dressed in her uniform that smelled of fajitas and rice, she lay down on the bed and held him for a minute. "Michael, I'll call you or send you an email probably tomorrow. Now, please rest." He nodded half asleep, and she took his head and lowered it down to the pillow.

She pushed herself off the bed, and as she did, a tear came from her eye, and she looked at him as she opened the door where the night still reigned, and then she closed it and was gone.

Her email came to him the next day. He already knew what it would say, but read it anyway.

Michael, you probably realize that we will not see each other again, or at least for a time, but I know that I am now a much better person for having met you. When we met, we were both wounded, hurt, but I hope much less than before. I know that I have healed a little bit. You are a good person, the first good man I have met, and I hope that I have been good to you as well. I am not the woman for you. I want you to find a woman who is as good as your wife was to you. She can never take your wife's place, but she can love you. I hope with all my heart that you find her. I also hope that I can continue to write to you and tell you of my life. If you say no, I will understand. I wish you well on your trip, a pilgrim, and that you find what you are looking for.

Vaya con Dios-Luz

He simply wrote back:

Thank you for your kind words. You are always welcome in my life.

That night, he packed up his belongings, and the next morning checked out of the motel, found the on ramp to Interstate 10 and drove east into the rising sun.

Interlude Two

As he drove across Texas and north into Oklahoma and Kansas, he realized that he had almost neglected two important dates. One was Thanksgiving. Usually he and Beatrice had Thanksgiving at their house and invited over not only the girls; Danae was home from college anyway, but friends as well. Beatrice enjoyed cooking, and went out of her way to make the day a memorable gustatory experience, with a huge turkey, mountains of mashed potatoes, vegetables, rolls, and desserts. Only the last one, when she was too ill and weak to do so, did she pass up on the holiday cooking. Laura cooked a much simpler meal for the four of them. He missed Beatrice's cooking; when he tried to imitate her recipes, depending on the ingredients, they came out somewhere between only fairly edible to not worth feeding to one's enemies. Beatrice had a touch with the kitchen that left him both proud and envious.

Now, he had Thanksgiving dinner by himself at a restaurant in Dodge City. It was one of the few in the city that was open; he drove around for almost an hour until he found a Denny's that was lit up and busy. The hostess and waitresses looked like they had been dragged from their families and homes to be there. As he looked around the dining room, he saw it full of older couples, or single people like himself, and he wondered if there was some truth in the adage that holidays are the loneliest times of the year. He wondered what Danae and Laura were doing, and when he returned to his hotel room, he sent a long email to them, saying how much he missed them.

They, in turn, sent him an email Thanksgiving card. At first, he did not know how to open it, and it took him a few minutes to figure out the logistics of the software. When he finally activated it, an animated group of turkeys sang a silly jingle that ended up with a Happy Thanksgiving message. He had to smile, and wrote back expressing his thanks and wishes.

He also almost forgot Beatrice's birthday. Birthdays are special days to remind people of when they first experienced the finite world and the years that have passed since. His own birthday was in April, so soon after Beatrice's death that he let it slip by without any real notice; he did not feel much like celebrating then. Danae had her twenty-first just before he left in late August; he took her out to dinner and gave her a bracelet that had belonged to Beatrice. She looked at it, remembered having seen it on her mother's wrist, and cried. Laura's was in September when he was in Arizona; he stopped at a flower shop in Tucson and arranged for a bouquet to be sent to her. With Beatrice, the past two birthdays were affirmations, still holding her own against the advance of the disease. She did not want any gifts, only that her family was with her on those occasions. Her birthday two years previously had been a joyous occasion; the chemo had gone well, her hair was coming back, and she could still walk four miles a day. As a present, he had taken her to the Monterey Bay Aquarium, one of her favorite places. She loved the three-story aquarium in the main hall, and also the Open Sea exhibit with its great loggerhead turtles and sharks. He patiently walked with her as she delighted in the jellyfish and delicate sea horse displays. Outside, on the back deck, they watched the tidal pools and gazed far out into Monterey Bay. That night, they celebrated her new year at a restaurant on the Fisherman's Wharf, and through the windows watched the lights of the peninsula reflected off the waters just beyond their table.

Her last birthday, though, was more somber. By that time, the tests showed that she had slipped out of remission, the disease was spreading, and she could walk maybe a hundred yards at a time before sitting down exhausted. They knew that there would probably not be too many celebrations left. And they were right. When he stopped in Wichita on the evening of November 30, he had a modest dinner, ordered a piece of cake, said Happy Birthday to her, ate it, and then silently cried.

December

"Michael!" Denise greeted him at the door, and then gave him a hug. ""Michael, it's so good to see you! Come on in out of the cold. You have to get used to St. Louis winters all over again." And she pulled him inside to a warm and artfully decorated living room.

"Denise, now that I can catch my breath, how are you doing?" He quickly looked over his beloved cousin, and she was as he had always known her: same long hair in a pony-tail, although now with threads of grey in it; same round wire glasses that used to be called granny glasses; same bluejeans and pullover sweatshirt; same expression of impishness on her face. She hasn't changed a bit since I last saw her four years ago, he thought, and in a lot of ways that's good.

As if Denise was reading his mind, or at least watching his expressions, "Yes, I'm the same as I always have been; did you really expect anything to be different?" And he smiled, "No, not really. Just keep being the way you always are, Denise."

"Come in the kitchen, sit down, I'll fix you some coffee."

He took off his jacket, hung it on the clothes tree next to the door, and followed her through the house. In the small but comfortable kitchen, he took a chair and she put the coffeemaker on the stove, then sat down next to him and took her survey, seeing the new lines below his eyes, the increased grey in his hair.

She took his hand in hers. "Michael, I'm sorry I didn't make Beatrice's service, I really am."

"Don't worry about it," he replied, "You called and wrote a very nice letter, that's what matters. Besides, you were out of the country. It would have been far too much to fly all the way from Italy to California and back. I wouldn't have expected you to do that, and I don't think anyone else would have either."

"Well, I still think I could have done more."

"There was nothing more that was possible. It's just the way things were. Now that it's over, don't fret over it. That's the way I look at it, although I've found it's not as easy as it sounds."

"I'm sure it's not. Well, if you don't mind, let's talk about happier things. How are the girls doing?"

"They're fine. Laura likes her teaching, and I assume married life, and Danae, I hope, is not letting the house fall to pieces while I'm gone. They're wonderful kids, I wonder how I would have even made it without them."

Denise looked him over again. "And how are you, Michael?"She stopped. "Well, maybe not. You've probably heard that a lot in the past several months. You can talk about it later. Now, what would you like to do while you're here?"

"What's your schedule? When do classes end for you?"

"I have to give my last final on the sixteenth, and then, of course, turn in grades. That shouldn't take long. Afterwards, I'm free until the middle of January."

"How have the classes been this semester?"

She shrugged. "My freshman writing class was the usual. Half the kids come in thinking they're still in high school. It takes about a quarter and some Ds and Fs to make them realize that they're not. I'm teaching a graduate seminar on Dante this semester. Good group, real sharp."

"Is that why you were in Italy in the spring?"

"Well, yes and no. I did do some research on Dante there, but really nothing that wasn't already known. A friend of mine in Florence told me about several new manuscripts dealing with the d' Medici family that were found in the archives at the Ufizzi. I was one of the first to study them. Interesting people. I'm thinking of eventually teaching a class on the d' Medicis and literature."

She gave him a playful nudge. "Michael, when you go back to the high school, which I assume you will, make sure they're prepared. I know that you probably do a good job, but remind your colleagues. These kids are coming to us like they never heard of essays and research papers, and their grammar and syntax are horrible. Hopefully you do better with them in California than the high school teachers do here in Missouri."

He grinned at his cousin; they had had this talk many times before. "Denise, you get the top ten percent of high school graduates at the university. We deal with the other ninety percent."

She looked at the clock. "Are you tired of restaurant food, and want a home-cooked meal? Or we can go to a little place I know only a few miles from here."

"A home cooked meal sounds fine."

"Good, then cook it yourself. You know where everything is. I cook maybe three times a week at the most, and I'm not about to break a streak just because my favorite cousin is visiting."

He laughed at her. "Denise, you really haven't changed a bit, have you? Still fighting the entire world and determined to win."

She gave him a mock warning. "Michael Lindstrom, as long as you're here, you're going to have to put up with a fifty year old single woman who's added menopause and hot flashes on to everything she was before. God help you."

He laughed again, and said, "Get your jacket. Let's go take a look

56

at this restaurant of yours and see if it passes muster. If I decide not to go back to teaching, maybe I can become a food critic."

The next day, while Denise was at the university, he drove to the riverfront. He wanted to see the new stadium, but he also longed to see the Mississippi River, the great moving body of water that essentially split the country into east and west. He knew it began as a small creek in Minnesota, not far from where his family also began, but by the time it reached St. Louis, it was more than a mile wide, carrying thousands of tons of water and silt south each day. Humanity began on riverbanks, he thought, the great cities of the world all sprang up on the shores of one river or another. He glanced at the Gateway Arch, rising 630 feet above the waters and the city. The first great adventure of the new country, the Corps of Discovery under Lewis and Clark, started only a few miles from here. The Arch, the Jefferson Expansion Memorial, commemorated it. Many years earlier, he had taken one of the capsules to the top of the Arch and looked down, first to the east, and then to the west and he saw, as a hawk or eagle or an owl would, the vastness that would become the United States. Afterwards, he preserved those images for a long time.

Another day, he wandered around the Forest Park area. He loved Forest Park; it was one of his favorite places when he was growing up. He would take the bus from Webster Groves and get off near the zoo; the zoo was free, and he would go often during the summer, spending all day walking through the animal houses and enclosures. He particularly enjoyed the aviary, with its multicolored international birds and their strange calls. If he tired of the zoo, he would go over to the art museum or to the science center with its planetarium. Like the art museum, the displays and exhibits fascinated him for hours. He often thought it strange that he was fascinated with art and science. He still liked those things, but history grabbed him in college; the past with its endless branches and connections and what ifs caught his imagination and never let go. At one point he thought, what if Beatrice and I had never met? Then my world might be different, our worlds might be different. Beatrice might have gone through cancer with someone else, or alone. The girls might have been the product of some other man, and their names might have been Samantha and Destiny, or Mary and Megan, or they might not have existed at all.

He first brought Beatrice to St. Louis the summer after they were married, to show her where he had been born and raised and spent his early years. She was introduced to Denise, who was still in college, and also his other cousins and aunts and uncles. With the exception of Denise, he never felt that close to any of them, but they were still family.

57

She enjoyed St. Louis, with its Midwestern greenery, the two great rivers, the Mississippi and the Missouri, and the flower gardens and parks. He took her down into the Ozark mountain region, to the Black River area in southcentral Missouri, where he had spent much time fishing and hiking as a boy, and she found it entrancing. He also took her down to Springfield, to Roaring River State Park, almost on the Arkansas border, another place where he had spent his early years. She loved hiking through the woods that delineated the park, and in the mornings, they sat on a hill overlooking the river and watched the trout fishermen in their waders and creels line up almost shoulder to shoulder in the water in the early morning light, waiting for the signal from the rangers. When the horn blared at seven a.m., they all cast their lines into the water in unison, afraid that the next angler might catch the choice fish. For some, the trout bit immediately; others kept flailing away until they hooked their fish or they gave up. He and his father had done the same thing once many years before.

Beatrice enjoyed the summers in Missouri; she adored the clear blue skies and the lush, almost tropical greenness of the trees and woods. However, a few times when they visited during Christmas break, she could never get used to the cold, the ice, and the occasional snow. The December weather stabbed her like a sharp-edged knife designed to maim, and she complained constantly about the freezing temperatures and chilling wind. She was a warm-weather person, and avoided going outside into the St. Louis winters as much as possible.

He also thought of what might have happened if he and Denise had not been so closely related, if they had become more intimate. After he and his parents moved to California, they constantly wrote letters to each other, long missives that put their thoughts and feelings into print once a month, if not more often. When they returned to Missouri during the summer, he and Denise would talk for hours at a time, never tiring of words, or of each other's presence. While they were growing up, Denise's brother and sisters used to kid her that she and he would get married someday. Besides the obvious fact that, as first cousins, they could not and did not wish to marry, Denise was far too independent minded to ever really settle down with anyone. Instead, she lived the life of a fussy and demanding scholar, teaching at the university and doing research in Medieval and Renaissance literature. That was her real love.

He remembered her phone calls late at night when he was in college and she was a teenager. They would talk for hours. Like many teens, she and her parents did not get along, and she would pour out to him all her anger and frustration about their rules and decrees and dictates. When she was not doing that, she would talk about her latest

58

boyfriend, or earlier boyfriend, or what it was like between boyfriends. He was a patient listener, qualities that would serve him well, especially when Beatrice was ill; she talked with him constantly, as if she was afraid she couldn't get everything out before she died. That was one thing he missed, he realized, as he strolled through the autumn brownness of Forest Park: listening to someone that he loved. After Beatrice's death, Denise, when she returned to the U.S., called him every week, sometimes twice a week, concerned about his health and his overall well-being. Denise was almost as good as Beatrice, he thought. He was lucky to have two wonderful women in his life.

When Denise's classes ended, and Christmas was still a few days away, they decided to take a quick trip to Chicago. He had not been there in many years, and enjoyed the roughness and immensity of it. Denise had a friend, an anthropology professor at the University of Chicago, and she took them around the city, to the areas and sights that tourists usually don't see. They finished the day in Lincoln Park, gazing out at the vastness of Lake Michigan, a Midwestern ocean that dwarfed the freighters and the sailboats that dared to cross it. "This is actually one of the most dangerous bodies of water in the world. Massive storms can blow up without warning, and ships can go down within a minute or two. The crew never even gets time to send a distress call," Karen told them. "The lake bottom is literally littered with vessels that never made it to port. "These waters have created widows for generations now, and I guess widowers as well," she added. They watched the choppy blue-grey December waters for several minutes, then returned to the warmth of the car.

On the drive back to St. Louis, Denise told him that Karen said they made a lovely couple, to hell with their cousin relationship, and should get married, now that he was single again. They both laughed.

Denise did not have a Christmas tree, which didn't surprise him. She was never one for ceremonies or religion, unlike him, who, when Beatrice was alive, attended church every Sunday. And, for a while after Beatrice's death, he continued to go, sustained by the spiritual strength that it offered. But since going on the road, he had not stepped inside a church building. Nevertheless, on December 23, he asked Denise where the nearest Lutheran Church was.

She snorted at him. "Michael, really, how would I know? You still don't believe in that, do you?" Only half-jokingly, she continued, "I thought you had grown up during all these years."

He knew that she was being open and sincere, and he did not take offense. "Nope, guess I'm still a child. Got to have some saving grace

59

sometime."

"Well, if you're that determined, I'll help you find one." A minute on the internet and they found Holy Family, only a few miles away. When he looked up the schedule, he noted the 9 p.m. Christmas Eve service and decided to attend it.

The next day, he went out, under the pretense of buying some food for Christmas Day. He had already bought presents for the girls and mailed them to California; this time, he went to a used bookstore that he knew of in downtown St. Louis, and bought two old literary volumes for Denise. One was a biography of Dante Alighieri from the 1920s; the other was a copy of Shakespeare's complete works from the New Modern Library. Once back at the house, he slipped through the living room, and hid them in his suitcase in the bedroom. Then he went to church.

The next morning, both he and Denise were up early. Denise was baking cookies; they had been invited to dinner at the house of a friend of hers, and the kitchen was full of warm oven smells. He watched her from the kitchen door. She had never been a good cook, but now he saw that she was quite proficient as a bakery chef. She had already made a batch of oatmeal raisin, and was now working on chocolate chip, out of a box, but better than store bought. He walked up behind her and reached around to take an oatmeal cookie. She slapped his hand with the comment, "You'll have to wait like everyone else."

"I thought I was special."

"Compared to who? Now, get out of here and go watch a football game or something. Isn't that what men do on Christmas Day?"

"At eight o'clock in the morning? I doubt it. Besides, I'm really not that interested in football. I know that makes me an anomaly, one of maybe one hundred males in the country who couldn't care less about football, but that's the way it is."

"Well, watch something. Otherwise, I'll make you sit down in a chair and be quiet, just like I do my nephews and nieces."

"Speaking of which, you have yet to mention your siblings. Are you still not getting along with them? I haven't seen or heard from any of them in years."

She put down the cooking spoons, turned to face him, and, with a sigh, replied, "You're not missing much. Actually, things have gotten better, but I still don't see them that often either. Kevin now lives in Springfield, Springfield, Illinois, that is, and has a real estate business. He just became a grandfather; his oldest daughter had a little boy in September. Margaret got divorced again about two years ago. That was

60

husband number three. It's been real hard on her kids. I feel sorry for them. She should just give up and live life on her own; it would probably be the best thing for everyone involved. I told her that and she really hasn't spoken to me since. Sharon, as far as I know, is still in Chicago; I don't hear from her much. Francis and her husband and children still live near Columbia. He got laid off a couple of years back and was out of work for almost a year. I saw the kids a lot then; she was working, he wasn't, and they were fighting, it seems like almost constantly. Several times the kids ended up spending nights here. Fortunately, it was during the summer when they were out of school, and so was I."

She looked at him with a sad resigned expression. "Somehow, Michael, kids today have it hard, more so than when you and I were growing up. You know, I have some of the best and brightest at the university, and they usually don't say anything about their backgrounds, but when I look at them in class, I can see all kinds of anguish beneath their faces. I just don't know."

"I do, I have a lot of them, too. Kids from broken families, houses where the parents fight all the time, or the dad hits the mom, or sometimes where the mom hits the dad, alcoholic parents, drug abuser parents. A few years ago, I had one student who was the product of her father's fourth marriage and her mother's third, and after she was born, her parents divorced and married again. I wonder how any of them manage to survive, but somehow they do. Sad thing is, they have baggage that they'll carry for the rest of their lives, I know that much."

Denise looked at him. "Have you heard anything lately from Susan or David?"

He answered, "I sent a letter to Susan in June saying I'd be back east around February or March. I didn't receive a reply before I left, but I've long since come to expect that. At least she knows I'm coming. As to David..." He shrugged his shoulders. "I have one slim clue that I'll follow up on. It may lead to nothing, but I feel I have to try. After so many years, anything is helpful. Can I ask how your mom is doing?"

"It's not better. I tried to talk to her on the phone about a week ago. She's in assisted living now, and slipping into dementia. She'll probably have to be moved to a specialized care facility in the next year or so. She doesn't yell at me the way she used to, so I guess that's an improvement, but she still won't accept me for who I am. Always thought I'd be the perfect little daughter: settle down, get married, have three or four kids, a husband who went to work every day and made all the money, a house in the suburbs with a white picket fence, a dog, and a cat. Well, I wasn't the perfect little daughter. Instead, she had four imperfect daughters, and one imperfect son. She could never understand that we're human beings like everyone else. But I guess I should be thankful; she still remembers me, or at least she did the last time I saw her. She doesn't know Kevin at all anymore, and she keeps getting Margaret's husbands mixed up. Margaret's been married so often that I do too. I'm going to drive to Columbia in a few days to see her. You don't have to come, but if you want to…I'll warn you, she probably won't recognize you."

"She's my aunt, my mother's sister. She's family, no matter what state she's in. I'll come."

She reached over, holding the cooking spoon in one hand, and with the other squeezed his arm. "Michael, it's so good to have you here. You're the one relative I can talk to without giving me the feeling I'm demented, arrogant, or degenerate."

"You better not say that, or the rumors will start floating around again." He quickly backed away to avoid a swat from the spoon. "I think I'll go see what's on TV. Maybe there's a parade or something."

He gave her the gifts shortly before they left for dinner. She was surprised and delighted, and admitted that she hadn't bought anything for him.

"That's okay, Denise," he said, "You're letting me stay here, and you listen to all my trials, and besides, I don't really need anything that I don't already have. I'm traveling light as it is. We'll go to dinner some night and call it even."

Before they left, she told him about her friends. "Shelia teaches art and art history at the university and her husband Paul is a financial consultant. It's an odd combination, I know, but they've managed to make it work for twenty-five years. They have one child, a daughter, Carmine, who's in college now, at Duke I think. I like her, she's kind of a free spirit. I see a lot of my younger self in her. I used to see her and talk to her a lot when she was still at home. Oh, you're not allergic to animals, are you?" And he shook his head. "Good, because they have three cats and four dogs. They're into animals. And Shelia said that some other people have been invited as well. I know a few of them, but not everyone."

Traffic on the highway was light on Christmas day afternoon, and they soon reached Lindberg Boulevard and Hazelwood. Denise drove the Prius (he realized, what other type of car would she drive?) silently down barren tree-lined streets until they stopped at a large two story white frame house with a spacious front lawn. Even though it was still wan daylight, the glow from the windows suffused through the air to where they were, and he could feel the warmth from them. He took the trays of desserts and followed Denise up the front steps to the door.

"Come in, come in!" came a call from inside. Denise opened the door, and was greeted by two small dogs and a fiftyish woman with long curly gray hair, deep grey eyes, and a lively whimsical face above a flowing scarf, purple blouse, and peasant skirt that came to her ankles. She hugged Denise, and then, to his surprise, hugged him as well. Oh, well, it's Christmas, he thought. "You are Michael. Welcome to our house on this day," she exclaimed. "Meet Sarafina and Eugenie." He looked around and didn't seen anyone, then he realized she was talking about the dogs. He looked down at them, and they looked up, tongues hanging down and tails wagging. He was reminded of a bumper sticker he once saw: More Wag-Less Bark.

"Come along," Shelia continued, and swept them along the hallway towards a back room. He noticed modernistic landscape paintings on the walls, and wondered if she had done them. They came out of the hallway and into a large expansive room with a high ceiling. One side was lined with shelves full of books and other knickknacks, one side had a fireplace where logs were burning crisply and more shelves, one side led to another hallway, and the fourth was almost all windows, looking out into a backyard with the greenest and most beautiful garden he had ever seen despite the snow and cold. He stared at it for a minute, almost forgetting everyone else in the room.

In the dimness he heard Shelia say, "This is Denise Thorton, my literature colleague from the university, and her cousin Michael. I don't know your last name..." "Lindstrom," he replied. "Michael Lindstrom, visiting from California."

She went on, taking his elbow, and leading him around the room. He now realized that there were about six or seven people besides Shelia, Denise, and himself. "Michael, this is my husband, Paul," and he shook hands with a large balding nondescript man about his age. "Our daughter, Carmine," a tall willowy girl with the same curly hair and grey eyes as her mother; "This is Barbara, who manages an art gallery." "Hello," he said to short plump woman about sixty; "Richard, who's in the art department with me," an Asian man in his forties with shoulder-length hair and a long mustache. He noticed that Richard was wearing sandals in December. He thought of the cold outside, but decided, to each his own. "Ruben, Carmine's friend," a tall thin bespectacled boy shook his hand hesitantly. "And Nora, a long-time friend of mine." "Nice to meet you, Nora." The woman was about his age, slim, bright green eyes gazing from a cherub face. He wondered if Denise were trying to set him up with one of them, then dismissed it. Denise wouldn't do something like that, he was sure.

He got himself a glass of wine and settled into a stuffed chair. Almost as soon as he did, an orange tabby jumped up on the armrest and stared, as if trying to intimidate him. He stared back at her.

"Well, hello there. Who are you?"

"That's Eliza, you're sitting in her favorite chair." said Carmine, walking by and picking up the cat, which squirmed in her arms, and, once put on the floor, immediately dashed off. "We have a couple of more. They're around here somewhere. Mom loves cats. She'd have a whole house full if she had her way."

"Eliza. The only Eliza I know is Eliza Doolittle from the musical *My Fair Lady*."

"Yes, and that was taken from George Bernard Shaw's *Pygmalion*. The old story about the artist who falls in love with his creation."

He was immediately impressed by her, and sat up.

"I hear you go to Duke. Are you home from school?" he asked.

"Not really, "she replied, almost defiantly. "I'm taking a year off. Mom and dad don't like it, but it's my life, not theirs. I just wanted to get out and around. I was in California, in Los Angeles, in October, I have a friend from high school who goes to USC."

"Carmine, how old are you?"

"Twenty-one."

He looked at her for a minute. She had a strong proud countenance, penetrating eyes, firmly set jaw, decisive smile which gave him the idea that she could handle most situations. She may have said she was twenty-one, but her whole expression said forty or older.

"Carmine, I think that at twenty-one you should be able to make your own decisions. I have a daughter who's your age, and right now she's taking care of my house and going to college. I've known a lot of young people over the years. Some of them are still real immature at twenty-one; others are grown up and ready to take on the world. You look and sound like you're one of the latter."

"Thank you, Mr....I don't remember your name, I'm sorry."

"That's all right. You just met me. Lindstrom."

"What do you do in California?"

"I'm a schoolteacher. High school social studies. I enjoy it. I like working with young people. I know you've probably heard this before, but I always tell my students that they've got to do what they like. What is your major, Carmine?"

"English. I'd like to go into writing or journalism. Mom and Dad tell me that, in these hard times, I should switch to something like

64

economics or business, but I just can't see myself doing that. It would be like a betrayal of what I really want to do."

"Well, your parents are right that these are rough times. But you're right, too; you should do what you really feel is best, for better or worse." He looked at her. "I'm sorry if that sounds hokey, but it's what I tell my students."

She smiled. "I wish you had been at my high school. I had a few good teachers, but most of them treated us like we were still third graders."

"Well, I've had some students who acted like they belonged in third grade. Others, though, were ready to go to college the day they entered high school. I deal with them as they are. You probably knew kids like that in your school, too."

She nodded. "I can think of some." She went on. "At least I'm in college now; people take you seriously there, or at least some do. I remember this one teacher in high school I never got along with."

"I hope he wasn't a social studies teacher."

She shook her head. "No, he taught art. Mom wanted me to take an art class, so, for once, I went along with her and did. Didn't work out."

"Why not?"

She shrugged. "This guy and mom knew each other, and he figured that I should have inherited mom's talent. I didn't. Art just isn't my thing. I ended up with wretched paintings of lakes, terrible fruit bowls, and awful, demented looking trees. Art sucks."

"Maybe they weren't horrible or terrible or awful. Maybe they were just your expression of how they were, that's all."

"No, they sucked."

He laughed. "I tried painting many years ago, when I was in junior high. They all looked grotesque, colors were bizarre, things like that. I never went back to art, and found out later I was color-blind. No wonder people gritted their teeth when they saw them."

It was her turn to laugh, a warm genuine laugh. "I like that. I'll have to write it down and use it sometime. It is okay if I put you in one of my stories? You'll be fictionalized, of course."

"Certainly," he replied. "Go ahead. That's what I always thought I was, a fiction." He asked her, "You say you want to be a writer. Do you do a lot of writing now? Short stories? Poems? Essays?"

She smiled, and he could tell that she was eager to talk about her work. "I've written a lot of short stories. I just finished one about a girl who goes to a college and then finds out it's not the right one for her. They're mostly about young people and what they go through. I've been

65

trying to get some of them published, but I haven't had a lot of luck so far."

"Well, don't give up. My wife was a writer, too. After she wrote her first novel, twelve publishing companies rejected it. She finally found one that was willing to take it. It just takes time and patience. There's a lot of competition out there."

"Your wife is a published author?"

"Yep. Three novels, and lots of short stories. So, keep trying."

A shadow appeared next to Carmine. It was Ruben, and she gave him a less than happy smile. She turned back to him and said, "Nice to have met you, Mr. Lindstrom."

She and Ruben disappeared from the room, and he got up out of the chair, more to stretch than anything else. He watched the people around him, his eyes moving from one to another. A minute later, Shelia's husband Paul came over and started talking to him. Paul discussed mostly his job as a financial planner, and how he helped people who were preparing to retire. Other than occasionally teaching economics to seniors and managing his own assets, Michael was not all that interested in financial planning, and even less interested in retiring from work. He listened politely to the man, occasionally murmured, "Yes, true, of course," when the occasion required it, but otherwise did not add anything to the conversation, and was glad when Paul was called into the kitchen to help with the food. The man was undeniably competent in his field, but otherwise totally boring. Maybe, he thought, Paul and Shelia were paragons of the notion that opposites attract.

"Come, Mr. Lindstrom," he heard a voice call out. It was Nora, whom he noted had previously been talking to Shelia's art professor friend Richard. "Dinner will be served in a few minutes." Other people were moving in the same general direction, towards the kitchen, and then beyond it. He had not noticed before, but another entryway led off the kitchen into an airy and spacious glass-walled and ceilinged room, almost like a hothouse, with a huge table at the center that was decorated with Christmas-themed flowers, plants, and ornaments. Above the table, he could see the bare trees against the now darkening sky.

The table had been set for at least twelve to fifteen people, and he now realized that several others had arrived after Denise and himself. Most of them were now gathered around it, or were coming in carrying bowls and plates of food.

"Here, Mr. Lindstrom, this is where you sit." Nora nudged him over to a place that had a card with his name on it; hers was next to his. He wondered if that was by accident.

Others were taking their places as well. He noticed that Barbara was seated next to Denise, and they were talking quietly, about art, he assumed. A young woman he had not been introduced to sat on Barbara's other side, and she was discussing something with Carmine. Ruben, Carmine's supposed beloved, was next to her, but he looked like he was left out of any of the conversations. The table was slowly filling up.

Then Shelia appeared. She stood at the head, tapped a spoon against her water glass, and announced in a loud voice, "Thank you everyone for coming on this special day. I drink a toast to all good friends and family, and may none of you ever be lonely, today, or any other day. Cheers!" She lifted her glass of wine and offered it up. People raised their glasses as well. "Now, let's eat," and she sat down.

Bowls and dishes immediately started to be passed around. He accepted mashed potatoes and cooked vegetables, then a platter of turkey and ham. Nora was busy, he noted, so to seem social, he started a conversation with the person on the other side of him, an elderly white-haired man whom he had not met before. The man turned out to be a professor emeritus of art at the university, and his interest was in Impressionism. He told him of a recent trip to Paris to study the works of Monet and Renoir at the Musee d' Orsay. "The Louvre is too full of people," the man commented with disgust. "I saw the *Mona Lisa* once, and never will again. No crowd control at all, just a mob, people shoving and pushing to get near it. On the other hand, the Orsay is dignified and quiet, the kind of atmosphere needed to appreciate great art."

The man was still declaiming about a new theory concerning Surat's Pointillist technique, when he heard a "Hmm," from next to him, and realized that Nora wanted some of his time. By now, the woman next to the retired professor was listening to his stories, and he turned his attention to the opposite side.

She began talking to him. "I heard you are a teacher. I was a teacher for a few years. Mostly fourth and fifth grade. I quit when I realized it just wasn't for me."

"Well, that happens sometimes. People find out they're more interested in other areas, or that teaching just isn't for them. We've had a couple of teachers at our school leave in the last few years for basically the same reason. What do you do now?"

"I work in the university business office. But I have other interests as well. "And she started in on her gardening and her love of antiques and her volunteer work at a local hospital and several other projects. He followed along as she gave what amounted to a resume of her activities, and between that and trying to eat and keep up with other conversations, managed to stay relatively interested in what she was saying. He assumed that she was single, and if he had been set up with her, based on her loquaciousness and apparent self-centeredness, he was not exactly going to encourage her.

The dinner went on for over an hour, with plates being passed back and forth until pretty much every dish was empty. When he saw people getting up to clear the table, he volunteered his services, but Shelia told him, "Nope, you're a special guest. Go sit down." He did notice that Nora had gone into the kitchen, and took the occasion to go back into the sitting room, to the same chair he had been in before. The room was empty and quiet, and he sat back and relaxed. Then Carmine came in.

"Mr. Lindstrom, can I talk with you some more?"

"Carmine, you're one of the few young people I've met, who, I get the idea, is more comfortable around older adults than their own generation. Has anyone every told you that?"

"Sort of," she replied. "Actually, kids my age bore me. They're into video games and Facebook and Twitter and all that crap, and girl drama and sports. When I'm around them, I feel like I'm back in middle school. It's even worse at Duke. All the girls care about is sororities and what boys to date, and all the boys seem to think about is playing football and fraternities and fucking, oh excuse me," he shrugged off her explicative, "girls. You get tired of that real fast. No one seems to care about anything *serious*."

"And what to you is serious?"

"Writing, poetry, theater, politics, helping the poor, social justice, just about anything that really matters. I know that probably sounds nerdy to you, but that's what I want," she announced.

"Carmine, I thought exactly the way you do when I was your age. Still do, to a great extent. That's one of the reasons I went into teaching. So I could help young people see the larger world. I like to think I've succeeded with at least a few. Most I'm not sure about. I'm not being facetious or condescending, I believe in those kinds of things as well."

She stared at him. "You do?" she finally replied.

He continued, "I do. And if you really feel that way, then you should go with it, and to hell with what everyone else is saying and doing." He paused. "I've said exactly that to my students, well, with the *hell* part left out." She smiled. "Trouble is, most of them are what you described, wrapped up in their own little worlds. It's hard to break through. I do the best I can."

She looked at him. "You must be an awesome teacher."

"I try."

"Why are you not teaching right now? I heard my mom say that

Dr. Thorton told her that you're kind of on a break this year."

"The same way you are?" She shrugged, and he went on. "I felt I had to get away for a while."

"What happened to you, then? The only thing I can figure out is that something traumatic happened to you. I can kind of see it in you, and also, I see that you're wearing a wedding ring, but your wife isn't here. So," she continued, "Something happened between you and your wife. I'm sorry if I sound like I'm prying into your personal affairs."

He gave her a long hard look. "You're not only mature, but very perceptive as well, far more than most other people, and for that I'm going to tell you the truth, which I probably wouldn't do with someone else your age. Fact is, my wife died nine months ago. Breast cancer."

"Oh." And she suddenly froze, then turned away, and he could hear faint sobs. A minute later, she turned around, and said, "I'm sorry."

He said quietly to her, "Judging by your reaction, you must have gone through something similar at one time. Did you know someone who died from cancer?"

She nodded her head. "My older sister. She had juvenile leukemia. I guess there are some types that are mild and can be cured, and others that are real bad. Anyway, she had one of the bad forms, and only lived about a year after it was diagnosed. She was ten when she died, and I was about eight. What made it hard was that we were very close. Ever since then, I've felt this kind of hole in me. I can deal with it, but it's always there."

It was his turn to nod. "Which is probably part of the reason why you're serious about wanting to help the world. You've known what one of the worst parts of it is, seeing someone you care for die."

"Is that the way you feel about your wife being dead, not here anymore? I'm sorry if I'm being too personal."

"No, not at all." He thought about the question for a minute. "Sometimes. We were married for thirty years. Sometimes I still think of her calling me or walking through the front door after a day at the school, or at night I wake up and expect her to be next to me but she's not. I'm slowly accepting it, but it'll take a while."

In the background, beyond the room, they could hear the bustle of plates being stacked and silverware being sorted and odd chatter, the sounds of a full house at holiday time. They stopped their conversation and listened to it for a minute. Then Carmine started up again.

"When Cyana died, I don't know if mom or dad ever mourned. Mom always had her happy smile bubbly face, and dad just went off to work. I don't think they've mentioned it in years. I guess, to them, life goes on. Whenever I try to talk to them about it, they just change the subject. It's like, to them, when someone's gone, they're gone, and that's it. Time to go on."

"Speaking of which," he looked around. "What happened to your friend Ruben? I would have thought that you wanted to spend time with him."

"Oh, him," she replied. "He's not really my boyfriend. He's a guy I knew in high school who had a crush on me. He's a nice guy and I like him, but that's about it. Mom invites him over on occasions like this; she probably thinks we'll get married someday. I know that mom means well, but she's not me. He left after dinner. Probably to go over to some guy's house to play video games or watch football on TV."

"Just like the boys you know at Duke."

She laughed at that one. "Yep, he'd fit right in. Except that I don't think he's ever slept with a girl, and he's not about to with me." She then looked at him with a shy smile. "You're a lot like Dr. Thorton." His face signaled surprise, then understanding. "I like talking with her. She doesn't talk down to me and she makes me feel like I matter to her. She's an awesome person. I hate it when adults talk to me like I'm five years old."

They head a muffled sound and looked up. Nora was peering into the room and looking at them. She focused on Carmine, and, in a tone of authority, told her, "Your mother needs you in the kitchen. You better go right away."

"Oh, ok." Carmine got up and left without a word. Nora sat down in the chair she had been occupying. He got the idea that Carmine wasn't really needed, but that Nora wanted to get her out of the way.

"I hope that Carmine hasn't been bothering you," Nora said with finality.

"Not at all. She's a mature and intelligent young woman. I enjoyed our conversation."

"She can be tedious. She's been kind of wild and rebellious; I think that Shelia and Paul spoiled her too much for her own good. Now, she's talking about not going back to school. We worry about her."

"You sound like you're as much a parent to her as her own parents are."

"I am. Shelia and I have been friends since high school. Since I never had any children myself, she's as much a daughter to me as anyone."

He sat up in the chair. "Carmine talked about having a sister who died young. Did you know her as well?"

"Yes, very sad. It's a taboo subject with Paul and Shelia. They just don't want to talk about it for whatever reason."

70

"Well, some people are like that when it comes to loss."

She looked at him. "Are you?"

"Did Shelia tell you about my wife?"

"Sort of. When she spoke to your cousin, it was probably mentioned. Shelia told me about it. You should have said something earlier."

He saw in her face something that he wasn't quite sure of, but didn't like, as if she were too eager for the details, too questioning. When he finally spoke, he didn't lie to her; he just didn't say everything. "I've had to explain it to so many people by now, it's just gotten kind of boring. I sometime wonder if I should just write up an explanation and hand it out to anyone who asks." He shrugged and continued. "I'm not near ready to meet or take up with anyone else, but I do want that wholeness that I used to have."

He saw the expression on her face suddenly change, knew that he had guessed right, that she had come to be set up with him. He thought Shelia was trying to set up her daughter, then her friend. Forget the past, the future is all that matters. He suddenly felt sorry, first for Carmine, and now for Nora.

He vaguely heard her talking to him. "How long are you going to stay in St. Louis?"

He thought for a second, then replied, "I'll be here until New Years at least; after that, I'm not sure. Probably move on within a few days. It's the new year, new life, turning over a new leaf, all that stuff. I think that I'll head east some more before heading back."

"I was told you used to live here. You don't want to come back, do you?"

He shook his head. "No, that's way gone. I have fond memories of growing up in this area, and it's good to visit, but my home's in California now. Denise has been enticing me to move back here, too. Won't work. I've been too Californiaized."

He heard the others heading into the kitchen. "Time for dessert? Let's go have some."

Later that night, when they were driving back to Denise's place, he told her about his conversations with both Carmine and Nora. She shook her head mournfully at the mention of the sister who died. "Yes, I knew about that, but Shelia and Paul have never talked about it to me. Carmine has, though. She really misses her sister." As to the encounter with Nora, she became disgusted and apologetic. "I'm sorry to have put you in that situation, Michael. If I had known that you were invited to be set up, I'd...Well, whatever. The evening's over. Poor sad woman."

He said, 'Who?"

"Nora. She's fifty, Shelia told me that. Never been married. Now she starts looking for a husband. Well, be glad you're away from her."

Later that week, they drove to Columbia, and Denise's mother was like she had said. The old woman, shabby and uncomprehending, bearing no resemblance to the aunt that he knew when he was younger, did not recognize him, and ranted about imaginary enemies the whole time they were there. He left almost in tears, and Denise commented, "Hopefully we won't end up the same way when we get to that age."

He and Denise were planning to go out to dinner on New Year's Eve. Then she got a phone call from a colleague at the university. "Oh, my God!" he heard her say. She said a few more things, then put the phone back on its stand and sat at the table.

"What happened, Denise?"

"Paul and Shelia Rickart were killed in an auto accident earlier today, just a few hours ago."

"Oh, that's too bad. I'm sorry to hear that."

"Drunk driver. Guy was celebrating early, I guess. Plowed right into them. Both of them died at the scene."

Denise looked at him. "Cousin, I don't feel like going out after all. Look in the refrigerator and see if there's something you can cook."

The phone rang again as he was starting to fix a makeshift dinner. Denise answered it. "Hello? Oh, hello!" She listened for a minute. "Of course you can. Come over and have something to eat. We're making dinner right now. Do you remember where I live? Good. We'll see you in a little while." She put down the phone. "Carmine, Shelia and Paul's daughter, is coming over. Set another place at the table."

Carmine knocked on the door twenty minutes later. Denise answered it and hugged her for a long time. Then he came over; he meant to take her hand in sympathy, but she hugged him as well, her tears flowing all over his shirt. Finally, he led her to the table, and motioned her to sit.

As they ate, Carmine's cell phone rang almost constantly. After the first half dozen calls, she put it on silent and continued her meal quietly. Finally, Denise asked her, "Where are your parents' bodies right now?"

"They're at the county morgue. I talked to the assistant coroner before I called here. He'll probably release them tomorrow sometime. I'm not sure what to do after that. Both mom and dad were only children, and all of my grandparents died years ago, so I don't have any close relatives, only some second and third cousins back east that I barely know and haven't seen in years."

Denise quickly took over. "I know a very reputable funeral home. After we're finished here we'll call it and tell them the situation. I'm sure they've dealt with this sort of thing before, many times, even on New Year's Eve. We'll get you through this, honey, don't you worry. Now, do you need a place to stay tonight, or do you want to go back home?"

He looked at Denise and listened to her with increasing admiration. When Beatrice had died, he was lost, even though, unlike this, he knew what was coming. He, along with Laura and Danae, had made the arrangements in a kind of stupor, pushed forward by fates that had propelled him every foot of the way to that moment.

The next day, even though it was New Year's Day, the three of them visited the funeral home, the preparations and services were made, and the obituary notice was posted. The funeral was held five days later in the home's small chapel. Neither of Carmine's parents had been in a church in years, but she wanted a religious service, and the funeral home secured a local minister who officiated. About seventy people were present, many of them, according to Denise, faculty at the university. Richard and the retired art professor were there. He saw Nora come in, but did not talk to her. He did not see Ruben. There were several men and women in business suits, colleagues of Paul's at the investment company, he assumed. He noticed that some of them were surreptitiously looking at their smart phones during the service and left as soon as it was over.

Afterwards, a small reception was held at Paul and Shelia's house. The dogs barked at the excitement and the cats ran all over the place. Carmine picked up one of the cats as she had done at Christmas. "Mr. Lindstrom," she asked, "Would you like a dog or cat to take back to California?" She smiled, for the first time since the deaths.

"Carmine, I already have a cat, a stubborn, independent, and ill-mannered one who might not like a new arrival. In fact, I know wouldn't like any new arrival. Besides, I won't be back in California for at least four or five more months. Thank you for asking, though."

When people had gone, and everything was cleaned up, and they were ready to leave, Carmine gave both of them Christmas ornaments from the tree. Then she hugged each of them.

"Thank you for everything, Dr. Thorton. I couldn't have gotten though without you. And Mr. Lindstrom, thank you as well. Can I ask you a favor?"

"Certainly, what is it?"

"Can I have your email? I want to keep in touch with you, send

73

you some of my stories."

Denise looked at him and grinned. Her face told him without saying it. As they were walking out to the car, she was still grinning. He turned to her. "Get that smile out of your mind. I'm an old widower; I wouldn't even remotely consider getting serious with someone younger than my own daughters."

"I know, I was just playing with you; I know hero worship when I see it. But it's a new year. Who knows what will happen? If you do meet someone, I have to approve her. Someone needs to watch out for you, Michael Lindstrom."

Two days later, he packed up the Toyota, gave his cousin a hug, and headed north to winter country.

January

Traveling through the white fog of winter, he made his way into the Minnesota forest land until he came to the town of Swensen, some one hundred miles north of Minneapolis/St. Paul, and only a short jump from Grand Rapids. Here, the trees on either side of the highway disappeared into the snowy maelstrom like benign and disoriented ghosts, their main function to serve as guideposts for the road. They lined up in rows and led him into the town, then, as he looked back, they vanished into the dark.

He had not been in Swensen for fourteen years, and before that, several years earlier. But he knew where the streets were, he knew the stores, and he knew the houses most of all. Even in the blizzard, he could navigate off of Main Street (every small town in the Midwest has a Main Street) to any one of the neatly laid out avenues that branched off it. In this case, he drove down Main Street, turned right on to Eighth Avenue and drove three blocks, his Toyota etching tire treads in the snow. On either side of the street sturdy framed houses white clapboard style, most with second stories, peered out of the gloom with glowing eyes from half shaded windows, signs of life within. Finally he found what he was looking for, a residence at the end of the street whose western view stared off into the vast obscurity beyond the town, over whiteness that stretched into the far distance, perhaps all the way to the Rockies. He stopped in front of it, stared for a minute while the truck protested the cold and snow, then drove on until he found a turn-around, and drove back to Main Street. There, at the edge of the town, were several chain motels. He checked into one of them, hauled his bags and equipment into the room, and relaxed while the snow fell outside.

By morning the snowfall had stopped, the clouds were retreating, and the sun was making an attempt to appear when he stepped outside the hotel room. The coldness was still there, though; according to a thermometer next to the office door, the temperature read -12° F; no wonder my parents moved to California, he thought. Out on Main Street, he could hear the snowplows coming nearer, and in a minute they drove by, huge beasts with metal jaws shoving everything out of their way. He walked out to the Toyota, brushed snow off its hood and windshield, and wondered if he needed the snow grips he had brought all the way from Madera. He wondered even more if the vehicle would even start in this weather. He opened the door, slipped into the driver's seat and commenced working on the ignition. It took him three tries, but eventually the engine turned over and gave a satisfying yell before settling into a quiet purr. He let it idle, warming up for several minutes before turning it off and putting the grips on the rear wheels. He then started it up again. With a few deft moves and some patient coaxing, he turned the car out of the parking space and moved forward into the snow-filled parking lot. In less than a minute, he was on the road, driving, carefully, but still creeping forward, the thud thud of the grips biting into the snow and ice behind him.

As he drove into the town, it looked different than the day before, now that the white screen was gone. Stores looked like stores, offices looked like what they were, and houses looked like they accommodated people and not the other way around. At each one were boys, or sometimes their sisters, shoveling or sweeping snow off the walks and driveways. A few snowmen had already sprouted in the front yards of some. Children had sleds out and were speeding down mini-hills in backyards; others were staging snowball fights with trash can lids as shields. Outlined against the white were dozens of shades of red and blue and green and brown and black jackets, caps, gloves pants, and boots. Here and there, dogs played; the larger ones sticking out, the smaller ones disappearing every time they jumped. He drove around the neighborhoods for some time, taking in the sights, trying to connect them to his own memory from decades before. In the shifting patterns of his experience, he found commonality, noted it, and kept it for future reference, which, for some unknown reason, he felt he would need.

He wondered if the children were still on winter break, or, because of the storm, were given the day off from school. As he turned the corner of one street, he came into view of the elementary school; lights were on and cars were in the parking lot; next to it was the high school, still small; he estimated that no more than five hundred students, including those bussed in from the rural farm areas, attended it. It was the "new" high school, built about twenty-five years ago to replace the old one. The old high school, no longer used, had burned down several years earlier, but he still had a photograph of it on the wall of his study, all brick and windows, when it was tall and strong against the Minnesota sky, with the plains in the background. Beyond the high school, he turned around again, and headed for the other side of town.

He found the house easily, unlike the day before, when it was almost lost in the blindness of the blizzard. By this time, the street had been plowed, and, between that and the chains, he roamed the neighborhood until he came upon it. He stopped the Toyota in the middle of the street for a minute and looked at it. Now he could view it clearly, and it reminded him of Sunday family get-togethers, holiday visits, vacation destinations, and, most of all, the passing of relations. This was where they would gather before the journey to the cemetery.

That kind of event had last occurred fourteen years ago, and shortly afterwards, his cousin, who had inherited the house, sold it. But, he could see, during the years, it had not changed much, aside from possibly a new coat of white paint. He noted the front door, and considered how many times he had gone through it, how many times it had slammed after him, how many times he had seen the last images of his grandparents, then only his grandmother, framed in it, then empty as he closed it and moved out into the yard.

He was idly musing these thoughts when a middle aged man came up and peered at him through the driver's window.

"You're interested in my house? Sorry, it's not for sale." He blurted out, making the statement seem half comical, half serious.

"Oh, I'm not interested in buying it," he replied. "I was just looking at it. I already know a lot about the place."

"How's that?"

"This is the house my father was born in. I spent holidays and vacations here." He looked directly at the man.

"You're serious?"

"I am. Does it still have the big front room, and the master bedroom behind the kitchen? Is there a door in the kitchen that goes out on to a screened-in back porch? Is there a small half bath underneath the stairs?"

"You do know this house," the man replied. "I'm John Sorensen. I bought this place about ten years ago. People who had it before me lived here only a few years."

He looked at the house and replied, "My grandfather built this house in 1922 and lived in it until he and my grandmother died. Then my uncle owned it, then my cousin. By the way, my name is Michael Lindstrom." He stuck his hand out the window to shake with the man.

"I've heard people here talk about the Lindstroms, but I don't think any of them are around here anymore. There's a plaque in the gym at the high school honoring a Robert Lindstrom, I've seen it; I work at the high school."

"That was my father's younger brother, the uncle who lived here," he said, "One year, I forget which, it was in the late '40s, he was All-State in basketball. He died a few years ago."

"Sorry to hear that. I coach basketball myself. Well, if you want to, come on in and take a look. It's better than sitting in a car when it's below zero out." John Sorensen swept a hand towards the house.

He hadn't intended to go through the place, only look at it from the exterior, but why not? The man was right, it was cold, and maybe he would benefit from glimpses of his past. He got out, and followed the man up the walk to the door.

Inside, he was immediately warm. His eyes swept around the room and took in the still sturdy hardwood floor, the walls with the built-in bookshelves, the rough-textured ceiling. Nothing had changed, but it had. A new sofa was against the far wall, a rocking chair in the corner, a clothes tree next to the door. Photographs of what he assumed were family members on another wall, and a large flat-screen TV next to the rock and brick fireplace. He was taking it all in when a woman only a few years younger than him came through the opening that led to the dining room.

"Marcia, this is Michael Lindstrom. His grandparents built this place and he grew up in it. He was just passing by and stopped to talk. This is my wife Marcia."

"Nice to meet you. I won't impose on you for long. It's been almost fifteen years since I was last in this area. I just wanted to drive by, and your husband invited me in."

"Please make yourself at home. It's a pleasure to have you here, Mr. Lindstrom. Does being in here bring back a lot of memories?"

"Quite a few. We would spend the Christmas holidays here," and he pointed to where the TV now was. "My grandparents would invite everyone, and my uncle and aunt with their children. My brother and sister and my parents. In the summer, I don't know how many times I went in and out that front door." He stopped for a second. "You know, what I remember most is that my grandparents didn't speak much English. If I listen hard enough, I can almost hear Swedish coming from the dining room and the kitchen. In those days, I could understand what they were saying pretty well. I'm not sure if I could now." He stopped for another pause. "My great-grandparents came to this area from southern Sweden around 1900." By now, two young people, teenagers, a boy and a girl, were also standing around him, listening to what he was saying. "Well, anyway. My family lived in in this area for almost a hundred years, until they either died or moved away."

He heard the girl say, "A hundred years ago? That's *old.*"

He laughed, and looked at her. "Remember sixty or seventy years from now, your grandchildren or great-grandchildren will look at you and say, 'you're old.'"

John Sorensen cut in. "Kids, this is Mr. Lindstrom. His family used to own this house. Michael, this is our son Kenny and our daughter Samantha."

"Hello," he said. "You sound like my daughters. Anyone ten years older than them is *so old.* Or my students. As far as they're concerned, a person who doesn't know what Snapchat and Instagram are is positively ancient."

"Here," said Mrs. Sorensen, "Take a look at the rest of the house. It's ancient, as you say, but we've tried to make it young." The little group in the living room split up and she took him through the dining room and into the kitchen. Despite the new stove and oven and an automatic dishwasher, it was as he remembered it, full of cabinets and drawers and the memories of aromas of Swedish pastries and meats. He not so much saw the past in the kitchen but smelled it. And, sure enough, the door at the back of the kitchen still led out to a screened back porch. He walked out on to it, and looked not at the place itself, but the view that went far out onto the prairie, now covered with snow, almost blinding without his sunglasses.

Mr. and Mrs. Sorensen showed him around the house, and each room evoked a different reaction. The boy's room was where his father and uncle had slept when they were growing up, and where he and his brother and his male cousins stayed when they visited; the girl's, where his aunt had her domain; the bedrooms upstairs, now TV and hobby and sewing rooms, all with a scent of the past, ghosts that had never left and were staying in case someone like him returned. Little by little family reflections came back to him until they were strong and evident and here and now, until they were more real than the present.

Eventually, he came back to himself and went downstairs. He thanked the Sorensens for their generosity, and told them he had to leave, that he had other places to visit and things to do.

Mrs. Sorensen invited him. "You will come back for dinner, won't you?" and he found it hard to say no, and agreed to be back. "Five p.m.," she said, "If you get lost, call our number, but it sounds like I don't think you will," and gave him a piece of paper anyway. He agreed and left.

He drove outside of town, wondering if the country roads were cleared. By this time they were, and he was able to travel Highway 43 west of the town out into the fields, now barren, except for a few shriveled corn stalks and naked disembodied trees, and covered with drifting snow. After about four miles, he stopped near the turnoff of a one lane gravel road that led to a deserted broken down farmhouse in the distance, its caved-in roof covered with white powder. Across from it was a barn with half of its side boards fallen down and great holes in the roof. Owls must be the only creatures living in it now, he thought. He stared at the derelict structures for a minute, then looked back and saw the town on the horizon, dark bumps and ridges against the blue sky and white snow. He wondered how long it took his great-grandparents, newly arrived, to travel all that distance to this vast and unknown area, what it was like to leave a heritage. He looked again at the crumpled buildings, that these were all that was left of their years of toil and sacrifice. He closed his eyes for a minute and heard Swedish in the distance again, then opened them, got back into the Toyota, and drove on.

That evening, he had dinner at the Sorensen's. He told them of his trip, and people he had met and the things he saw. He launched into stories about visiting and growing up in the house, the adults eating at the big round oak table in this same room, and the children eating in the smaller breakfast room off the kitchen. He remembered that when a young person was old enough, he or she was allowed to sit at the big table, and he and his cousins waited every year to see if they would be chosen to eat with the adults. He mentioned, with a smile, that if the kids didn't like the food that was served, once the adults were gone, they would sneak out the back kitchen door and feed it to the dogs that were waiting on the back porch. After dinner, he and his cousins would crowd into the dining room. Extra chairs were brought in for them, and they would listen to their grandfather tell stories of his own parents arriving from Sweden and starting anew and himself growing up on the farm outside of town. Or how he met his wife, their grandmother, while attending the Lutheran church summer picnic in town one Sunday. It was late at night by the time he finished, but it was so far north that the sky was still light at ten p.m., so they went outside and played some more. He related how, during the summer, he and his brother and sister would ride their bicycles down the highway to visit the farm, which by that time was run by their great uncle, their grandfather's brother. Sometimes his grandchildren were there, and they would all get together and run through the fields, or bother the cows and scatter the chickens, or hide under the hay in the barn. Again, he paused and closed his eyes and thought about the ruins that he had seen earlier in the day, and tried to merge them, and could not.

Afterwards, he again thanked the Sorensens, and gave them his address and phone number and e-mail and invited them to California. They acknowledged that they had never been further west than Yellowstone, but that they would try to make it out West sometime. Mrs. Sorensen hugged him, and Mr. Sorensen and the two children shook his hand and then he left. It was January, and since the sun disappeared at four p.m., the sky was as dark as he had ever seen it.

He slept in the next morning, and did not get out of the motel room until almost ten a.m.. He had already decided that he would leave the next day, but there were still more things he wanted to do while in town. He had breakfast first at the diner next the motel, and then went down the street to the hardware store and bought a broom and some cleaning towels. He put these in the back cab of the truck, and drove down Main Street once more. By now the streets had been cleared of snow and he no longer needed the grips, but still had to watch for ice. He drove slowly to the eastern edge of town, until he came to the Lutheran Church with its whiteboard sides, tall thin spire, and long arched windows. A set of snow-covered wooden stairs fixed with railings that ran up to the doors, and next to them a bulletin board held the service schedule. He, though, was not interested in going inside at the moment. He took the outline of an otherwise stone path along the side of the building to the back, where a fence with a gate awaited. In a minute, he was through it, and among the gravestones.

Like many immigrant peoples in the Midwest in the 1800s, Swensen's Swedish Lutherans believed in burying their dead next to the church in which they worshiped their god. Pushing aside the snow, he walked among the stone markers and glanced at names and dates. Nystrom 1868-1940; Olsson 1895-1967; Petersson 1900-1970; Frisk 1898-1920; Berg 1875-1930. As he wandered through the cemetery, the names came by in flashes and then sparked out. Finally, towards the rear fence, he found what he was looking for. A section labeled Lindstrom, with several stones to mark the generations. Goren, 1878-1946-his great grandfather, and Erika Olsen 1879-1954, his great grandmother, both from Lund, Sweden; Jan, 1902-1979, his grandfather's brother who worked the farm after his parents died; Stefa 1900-1981, his wife; Karl, 1900-1976 and Anna 1902-1980, his grandparents; Ola Karlson 1905-1985, his grandfather's sister; Michael 1921-1923, his father's older brother who drowned in a creek at age two, and whose name he was given; Emma 1926-1931, his father's younger sister, a victim of measles; John Lindstrom 1955-1985, a second cousin who died from a drug overdose; and then, at the end, Stephen Lindstrom, 1924-1998. He stood, looking at the marker for a minute, then turned to his tools.

"Hi, Dad, I'm back," he said quietly.

He did what he came to do. With the broom, he swept away the snow from the markers and cleared a path to them. Then he took the towels and a bottle of detergent and began cleaning them until all the mud spots and the matted leaves and the weather stains were eliminated and they glistened in the January sun like newly polished cars. He looked from one to another, the grey marble against the snow and the picket fence and the flat land beyond it. He knew that this might be the last time in many years, perhaps the last time ever, that any of his family would visit the graves. His cousins and their families were all scattered, apparently too busy, perhaps too disconnected from the family legacy to come here anymore. As he watched over them for one more time, he shed a tear, or maybe it was holding back the glare of the light and the white from the snow.

He approached his father's grave once more, and rubbed his hand across the top of the marker. He thought of the day when the family had gathered here one last time, to lay his father in the earth. Stephen Lindstrom had died from a stroke near Sacramento, California. He received a phone call from his mother one day, saying that his father had gone into the hospital with heart problems. By the time he arrived in Sacramento, the old man had had a massive stroke, and lived only a few hours afterwards. His mother had originally wanted the body cremated and the ashes scattered, but his father, according to instructions found on the desk in his study, insisted on being buried in the town of his birth next to his ancestors. He had traveled from this community to St. Louis, from there to Europe, then back to St. Louis, and finally to Sacramento. Along the way he married and raised three children. Michael was the youngest. Before they moved to Sacramento when he was fourteen, the family spent almost every summer in Swensen, and the ancestral influence was imprinted into the boy, the origins of his genes and the meaning of his culture fixed him into what he would eventually become. Michael, more than his siblings, and probably more than his Lindstrom cousins, absorbed and remembered the stories told by his grandparents, and later his father and his uncle and aunt. His upbringing, he eventually realized, was in Missouri and later California, but his real inheritance began in Swenson and emanated out to everywhere he lived.

Here, too, he thought of Beatrice. The graveyard and the church brought back stories in which she had played the principal role. He had grown up in the Lutheran faith and could not remember a Sunday when he did not attend church with his father. Beatrice, though, was devoutly Roman Catholic, as were most Portuguese, and before they married they discussed their religious preferences. They eventually decided to get married in the Catholic Church in Firebaugh that Beatrice had attended since she was born. Afterwards, they each went to their own services. When the girls came along, she took the responsibility for their religious upbringing. They respected each other's faith, and never tried to convert the other. One Sunday Beatrice came home from church with the girls and told him of what happened when the service ended. They were leaving when one of the nuns came up to her and said, "I've noticed that your husband doesn't come with you." Beatrice replied, "Oh, he's not Catholic, sister." to which the nun said, "Her must come and see our church and find the way." Beatrice, knowing that the woman was being sincere and not wanting to offend her, said simply, "Thank you, sister, but I don't think it'll work out." Nothing more was ever said about him joining her church.

Eventually, he turned around and slowly walked back through the graveyard to the entrance gate. The sun had gone behind a cloud, and a brisk wind had picked up, causing the loose snow to fly and sting his face, and he zipped up his coat and put his hands in his pockets to ward off the chilling cold. His ears, too, were suddenly chilled, and he took out a cap from his pocket and put it on. He walked around to the front of the church, looking down, and almost bumped into a man coming from the parking lot.

He looked up and quickly jumped out of the way. "I'm sorry," he said, and then realized that the man was wearing a clerical collar under his black coat. With this recognition, he quickly repeated, "Sorry...Father," and gave an embarrassed smile.

The minister scrutinized him; he was a much older man, probably well past seventy, but he still had an air of spirit and energy about him. "For some reason, I recognize you, or I've at least met you before." He peered again into his face.

He remembered who the man was. "You officiated at my father's funeral many years ago; his name was Stephen Lindstrom," he said. "I'm Michael Lindstrom. I was just visiting my family's graves. I haven't been here in a while."

The minister spoke out. "I'm Reverend James Berg. Oh, yes, the Lindstroms. I remember them well. Your father was a few years older than me. I graduated from high school with his sister Monica in 1950. I remember going over to her parents' house on occasion. Good people."

"My Aunt Monica lives in Orange County, in Southern California, now. She and her husband moved there over forty years ago. I see her every now and then." He thought for a minute. "If you're Aunt Monica's age, I'm surprised that you're not retired by now."

The minister smiled. "I know. I turned eighty five months ago. When I entered the ministry in the 1950s, I took a pledge to serve the Lord and His church. True, I could have retired a long time ago. But my wife died in 2003, and I decided to stay active as long as I can. It makes me feel like I'm doing something useful, taking care of my flock, as the Bible says."

He motioned. "Here, come inside for a few minutes. Get warmed up." He took out a key, walked up the steps, and unlocked the door. They walked into the interior, and he gazed around the room with its rows of plainly furnished pews, the altar and the cross hanging behind it, the organ in the corner, and the pulpit standing out like a great pointed hand. He looked up at the steeply slanted ceiling with its unpainted beams and boards, and the light fixtures hanging down. This was a familiar scene, one he had witnessed every Sunday during the times that his family had visited, and the marriage ceremonies, and the funerals. What struck him, though, as it had every time he entered since he was small, were the windows on the side, allowing light to pour in on the congregation, anointing them in glow, giving them a communion that was even greater than that of the bread and wine. It never ceased to amaze him that in its simplicity this building in the community of his ancestors, defined his faith and his family. As long as it stood, he found home and life, and would always come back to it, no matter where he lived.

The minister seemed to read his thoughts. "You're back home again, aren't you? I get that same look and expression from people who have left this town, then return. It's not quite the same anywhere else. "

He replied, "About ten years ago, I was in Rome, and, among other places, visited St. Peter's in Vatican City. It was beautiful and overwhelming, but it doesn't compare to this, the sense of immediacy and intimacy, I guess, is what it is."

Reverend Berg nodded. "Yes, I too have been to St. Peter's, and felt the same way. Even when I went to Martin Luther's house in Germany and saw the church in Wittenburg where he posted his Ninety Five Theses, I felt like that. That may have been where our faith started, but this is where it is now. Put simply, it's like the old saying, I know it's kind of a cliché, but it still works: 'There's no place like home.'"

"So true."

"How long are you going to be staying here?" the minister asked. He told his story with only a few pauses, and leaving out only the more personal details. The man expressed his condolences over Beatrice's death, and invited him to stay until Sunday for services. He thanked him, but expressed his regrets that he had to move on, that other voices were calling him, other urgencies were at hand. They talked for a few more minutes, and then the minister said that people would soon be arriving to ready the church for a wedding that afternoon. They shook hands, and the man told him, "You are always welcome here, you are always part of this faith community, no matter where you live."

Before he left, he wandered back to the cemetery once more, gazed at his father's stone, brushed away a leaf that had fallen on it in the interim, and returned to the Toyota.

Interlude Three

He remembered his father vividly; a quiet very precise man who worked hard and expected everyone else to do the same. After graduating from high school, Stephen Lindstrom entered the military, and trained at Fort Leonard Wood in central Missouri; on weekends, he and other soldiers took the bus up to St. Louis, where he met Barbara Kessler, whom he would eventually marry. In 1944, he was shipped overseas, came ashore on Utah Beach on D-Day, and fought his way across Europe until Germany's surrender. Leaving the Army in 1946, he returned to St. Louis, and married Miss Kessler. Their honeymoon, it turned out, was a three day camping trip to Meramac State Park, about fifty miles southwest of the city. It was only three days because classes started at Washington University in four days, and his new job at a gas station started in five days. The first four years of their marriage, he worked full time, went to school full time and fathered two children. When he finally received his engineering degree, he quit the gas station and went to work for a construction engineering firm, helping to design and build highway overpasses and cloverleafs. For years after he was born, he knew that his father was not home at least a few nights every week; he did not know what for until he was in junior high school-the man had gone to graduate school at night and earned a master's degree; eventually he came to realize that when the family got together in Swensen for reunions, his father had more education than all of them put together. At first, he wondered what it was for; after all, as far as he knew, lots of people had college degrees. Then he understood that there was a purpose behind it. One night his father came home and told him that they were to be moving-and not just around the block; they were moving to California, to a place called Sacramento, wherever that was. His father had accepted a job at a junior college near there, teaching mathematics. At first, he was stunned; why leave? This was his home, the St. Louis area was all that he knew, his friends were there, his cousins were there, especially Denise, whom he was able to see on a regular basis. He rebelled for a few days, then resigned himself to it. Afterwards, he worried, not about himself, but what would happen to his brother and sister when he moved.

David was thirteen years older than him, more of a surrogate parent than a brother, and completely different from his parents. Where they saw opportunity and freedom, he saw oppression; where they believed, he was a doubter; where they thought of order and discipline as virtues, he saw them as vices. David had been a bright student in school, and had attended the University of Missouri after graduation, but he turned, in his parents' terminology, "radical," caught up in the anti-Vietnam War movement of the '60s. He blasted Monsanto and Dupont as child-killing pollution spewing capitalist war machines. He took up marijuana, grew his hair down to his waist, and dropped out of college. Within a few years, David was sequestered in a hippie commune in Ohio, and wanted nothing to do with his evil humanity-hating parents.

Susan was, in a different way, even more rebellious. She was her father's darling, shared his eyes and determination, and as a child and a teen saw the future like a far-reaching visionary. She was at the top of her class in every subject, was ASB vice-president, valedictorian, and set her sights on the best eastern schools. She ended up going to Bryn Mawr, but it didn't last long. During the winter of her third year, she met a boy who had flunked out of Penn State. He was feckless and unreliable, into alcohol and drugs, but he charmed her like no one else ever had. Within a month, she was spending most of her days and nights at his apartment and failing all her classes. Her parents made a trip to Philadelphia to plead and get her back on track, but she ignored them, and shortly before the spring semester ended, she dropped out, and she and the boy got married in a justice-of-the-peace office in Vermont. She never returned to school.

For the next several years, Susan and her husband drifted from town to town and job to job. They argued and fought; they drank; they eventually had a child, a daughter, thinking that she would help their marriage; but instead they slowly devolved into wretched excesses. Over time, she realized that she had made a mistake, but it was too late. She had become a sad shell of her former self, a rare mind lost to passion, impulse, denial, and stubbornness. While he grew up, went to college, married and raised a family, she wandered, drank, divorced her first husband, married again and had a second child, divorced and married a third time, and settled into life as a grocery store cashier.

It saddened him that his siblings threw away all that their parents had built up for them, but they were adults and had to forge their own way; there was nothing that he could do about it. He had sporadic contact with Susan, heard from her once or twice a year, but she kept to herself, and, based on what little she told him, was too ashamed to admit the morass into which she had fallen. He was certain that alcohol had deadened her, destroyed her self-worth along with her intelligence and vision. Maybe she no longer saw him as a brother or even a blood relation, simply as a person, a near-stranger who occasionally sent her messages of concern and sympathy.

As for David, he had disappeared altogether. Sometime in his mid-twenties he stopped communicating with his parents and as far as anyone knew, everyone else in the family. After he left the commune, he never sent a forwarding address or phone number. Over the years, David did not come to any family events, and he did not attend his father's and mother's funerals. No one had any idea of where he was, or even if he was still alive. Then, two years ago, a cousin who was visiting Buffalo, New York, on business, happened to eat in a restaurant where he was working, and despite the passage of time, recognized him. The man first denied he was David Lindstrom, but eventually acknowledged it, and shortly afterwards went in the back and did not come out. His cousin gave him the name and address of the place, but when he called it a few months later, he was told that David Lindstrom had quit.

Michael often wondered what had happened to those two, and why he was the one who was not affected by it. Why had they, who started out so full of energy and hope, turned out to be so burned and scarred, at least in the case of his sister, damaged almost beyond help? He could not think of any answers, knowing only that he had somehow escaped the flames.

February

On the first of February Michael arrived in Buffalo, New York, on one of the coldest days of the year.

He had spent the previous week in Montreal, visiting another cousin, John Reinsford, the son of his Aunt Monica, who had married a French-Canadian girl some twenty years before, and had lived in Canada ever since. He had not seen or talked to John in several years, and had not been that close to him at all. They had known each other from visits to their grandparents' house in Swensen, but afterwards retreated back into their own separate worlds once the encounters were over. So the visit was more of a courtesy call than anything else. He feigned politeness and "Good to see you again" wishes to people that he hardly knew. He told his cousin of the visit to the church gravesites; the man nodded and replied, "Yes, I'll have to get there someday," both of them knowing full well that he never would. They said goodbye with equally feigned salutations that they would see each other again, but both well aware that it would probably not happen, or at least anytime soon. So he did his family duty and moved on.

Now he was in Buffalo, a sprawling industrial city along the banks of Lake Erie, and south of Niagara Falls. In summer, Buffalo was a place that could be tolerated, but in winter, it was devastatingly cold, in some ways even colder than Minnesota. The icy wind that formed over the lake swept through the city, turning everything in its wake into ice and snow. He had been given warnings: several car accidents on the highway from Toronto across the border and down the river to the city. He did not want to be added to them.

As before, he found a small but reasonable hotel to stay at, and moved in for what he saw as several days, maybe up to a week or two, sojourn in the area. He rested overnight, and prepared for what he saw as an exhaustive and time-consuming process, that of finding the whereabouts of his brother David.

The first place to search was the most obvious-the telephone book, although he doubted there would be any real clue in there. Nevertheless, he opened it to the "L" section and looked for a David Lindstrom. There were, in fact, several Lindstroms, and one a "D. Lindstrom." He immediately called it, and quickly learned that the "D" stood for Deborah. He muttered his apologies and just as quickly hung up. On the offhand chance that his brother had a Facebook account or an email address, he trolled the internet one evening, but again came up short. He realized that the man could have changed his name, which would make it even harder. On an even more offhand bet, he decided to visit the diner. It had been two years since his cousin's sighting, but he decided to take the chance.

The place was a storefront cubbyhole, older, but clean, with a counter and ten tables with red and white checker coverings. It was afternoon, after the lunch rush. He asked for the manager, and a young woman about thirty came out from the back room, and peered suspiciously at him, as if he were delivering poison. As he explained his reason for being in the place, he saw the otherwise bland eyes of the woman come to life.

"I think I remember you calling. Yeah, David. I knew him. Older man, tall, pretty thin. His hands and face were pretty worn, as if he had been out in the sun a lot. I had no problems with him, he was a good worker actually. Never said much about himself, though. Nothing about his family, friends, anything. Real odd, but some people are like that. He was here for about a year, then gave his notice. Told me he had found another job somewhere else that was closer to where he lived."

He asked, "Did you have an address for him?"

The woman looked at him suspiciously again, and then relaxed. "You know, we're not supposed to give out information like that." She thought for a second. "Do you have some I.D. to prove you really are who you say you are?"

He took out his driver's license and also his school I.D. card. She looked at the pictures on both, looked up at his face, then looked again. "Boy, you really could be his brother. Give me a minute." She went into the back, then came out with a piece of paper. "Here," she said, "This is the only address we had for him. And this is a phone number. The prefix makes it look like it's a cell phone, so I don't know how reliable it is. But it's the best I can do for you."

"Thanks," he said sincerely. "I'll see where this leads. I appreciate it a great deal."

"Good luck," she said, starting into the back again. "And be careful driving around in this weather and ice. Be real careful." She disappeared.

As soon as he was out of the diner, he tried the phone number. As the woman had suspected, the number was a cell phone, and an electronic voice politely explained that it had been disconnected. Well, so much for that, he thought to himself.

The address was a different matter. That night, he looked it up on Google Maps, and found it to be in an area in the south of the city, low income, maybe not safe. He wanted to try it anyway, and the next morning drove among boarded-up houses and run-down apartments. People stared at him, perhaps noticing the California license plate.

Finally, he found the address and stopped at an apartment complex that was a bit better than the others. He thought, I've come this far, and carefully made his way to the second floor. There he found number 28 and knocked on the door. No one answered. He knocked again, and this time could hear movement inside. A curtain parted for a second, then fell back into place. Finally, a lock slid and a door handle turned, and he was looking at a fiftyish woman, who, despite her surroundings, exuded an air of presence and dignity.

"Yes," she said, "How can I help you?"

"Ma'am," he replied, "I'm looking for a David Lindstrom. I was told that he lived here until recently."

He noticed the change in the woman's face, morphing from guardedness to astonishment, and then as quickly, as if a plate covered it, to blandness. Like the woman in the diner, she was silent for a minute. Then she spoke haltingly.

"Why do you want to see him?"

He looked at the woman intensely. She had loosely arranged semi-grey hair that looked as if it had been luxuriant brown at one time. Her eyes were like the lake that lay beyond her dwelling, shimmering blue and open and disturbed, and he could tell that she was guarded in some way. Whether it was David or someone else who had caused it, he did not know, but he decided to answer her.

"I'm his brother, Michael Lindstrom. I haven't seen him in over thirty years, and I'm trying to find him now."

The plate fell down and landed at her feet with a crash. She stared at him, and then motioned, come in, without saying a word. She led him to a kitchen that was old, but neat, and gestured him to sit down at a small round table in the corner. She asked, "Would you like something to drink? Coffee, perhaps?"

"No thank you, I've already had breakfast. I'm fine."

"Here, have something anyway," and she handed him a glass of water. He accepted it, and took a sip. Like the water in each town he had visited, it tasted different, but that was all. It was just something to get used to. He sipped it while she sat down in a chair on the opposite side and quietly watched him, as if she were trying to find a resemblance in the face or the mannerisms. Finally, she came to a decision, and spoke again.

"What do you want to know about David?"

He replied carefully. "I want to know first of all where he is, and hopefully meet him. He dropped out of our family when I was a teenager. All I know is that he went off to college and became completely different, and then he was in a commune or camp of some kind. Afterwards, apparently he didn't want to see or talk to us anymore. The last I heard from him was when I was about fifteen or sixteen. Since then, it's just been second hand stories and rumors."

She nodded and stayed silent for another minute. Then she slowly spoke. "In the commune I was known as Sister Morning Bear. That's not my real name of course, it's Jane Andrews. But David and I had commune names. His name was Brother Skyhawk. We lived in a tent, the two of us, for about three years. Then the commune split up and we wandered."

"Where did you meet him, Jane?"

"At Mizzou. We took a couple of classes together and got to know each other. After a while, like a lot of college kids, we started talking about our lives and families. Eventually we ended up going out and then living together. We took a lot of drugs: marijuana, LSD, other stuff. Eventually, we decided to get away from life totally, and hooked up with this group in Ohio that we had learned about from some other students. They lived in teepees in the woods and shared everything. We were into the Back to Nature thing. This was the mid-late '60s, anti-war, anti-establishment, rebel against the system idea. No phones, no running water or bathtubs, TV or anything like that."

She had difficulty expressing some of the terms, at times her voice was slow and drawn-out, and he wondered if she had been damaged by drugs or maybe some other experiences, or perhaps she was just nervous by the unexpected interruption in her life, but he let her speak on without comment or interruption.

"We were called the December People; I heard that it was because the group had originally been founded in December 1965. Members came and went; most stayed about a year, although there was a core group that had been together since the beginning. As long as you contributed something you could stay. The group didn't like freeloaders, although there were always some of those. Mostly people contributed money. David and I both had some that we had saved while in college. We gave it to them and they let us stay."

He nodded, and asked, "And you said you lived with them for about three years?"

"I think it was about that time. It may have been a little bit longer."

"What did you do there?"

She put her hands to her head and thought for a minute. "We did some farming, we had, I don't know, about twenty acres of land for crops: corn, lettuce, tomatoes, carrots, some other vegetables. A lot of us worked in the fields. Funny, I grew up near Kansas City, never been on a farm in my life, and yet I learned how to farm. I never found out where all the land came from or who owned it. Some of the group worked at jobs in a nearby town. They had to dress fairly nice and keep their hair short. Most of the guys grew their hair long, and we wore whatever we wanted. If people wanted to go around naked, they did. Most of the children rarely wore clothes."

She was wandering, and he wondered again if she was having difficulty. He stopped her.

"What does David have to do with all this?"

She was quiet again, and after another minute resumed. "Did David ever tell you why he left his family? Why he didn't want to see them again?"

"Not to me, no. I was almost fifteen years younger than him. If he told my parents, I never knew about it."

A grey look came over her face, and again she was quiet. When she finally spoke again, she said, "Then I don't know if I should be the one to tell you."

"Why is that?"

"Are your parents still alive?"

"No, they've both been dead for a number of years."

"What did you know about their marriage?"

"No more than any other kid probably knows about his or her parents. They seemed to be happy, although there were times when they were kind of quiet, really didn't speak to each other a whole lot."

Jane nodded, and her face became even darker. She was silent once again. He pressed her. "What do you know about my parents? Or what did David tell you about them that I don't know?"

She spoke once more, softly, barely audible. "I will only say what David once told me and nothing else. While they were married, your mother had a baby by another man. She had an affair with someone else and it resulted in a pregnancy. It was after your brother and sister, and apparently before you. David said he remembers your parents having arguments, and being separated for a long time."

He realized he was holding his breath, and then he let it out in an explosion of air. He had never heard of this; no one in the family, anyone in his family, had ever mentioned this. None of his aunts and uncles, older cousins, other relatives. It came to him as a tsunami, overwhelming his mind, mad images rampaging through it, thoughts tumbling every which way.

"David told you this?"

"Exactly this. He said it was the main reason he cast off from your family. He couldn't stand the cheating, the lying, the hypocrisy. He

92

never wanted to see your parents again, especially your mom. He said your sister was especially hurt. When your parents had finished arguing, she would come into your sister's room and yell at her and sometimes hit her, saying she was cursed to be a girl, that the world had it out for girls, that they were good only for babies and cooking. Anyway, when your brother turned eighteen and went off to college, he swore that he would never be involved in the family again. That and the war and turned him off to the family. He told me all this one night at Mizzou just before we took off for the commune."

He sat back and thought about things. The revelation would explain why his parents suddenly moved when he was in school, why they were somewhat distant to each other at times, why they rarely talked about their married life before his birth. There had been a great breach of trust, of fidelity, of intimacy. It could explain why they sometimes took separate vacations for many years. It might also explain why his father wanted to be buried in Swensen, while his mother asked that she be cremated. There had been a gulf in their relationship.

He suddenly thought of a time, when he was about fifteen, when he had been in California for about a year, and he and his father had gone on a camping trip to Tuolumne Meadows in Yosemite. They fished and hiked during the day, and at night, walked out into the meadows, away from the lights and the campfires, and gazed up at the nighttime sky with its thousands of stars blazing in the deep. His father pointed out the Big Dipper and Cygnus and Aquila, and far overhead, Hercules. He asked his father something that he hadn't thought of until then: "Why didn't mother come with us?" The older man replied, "Oh, your mother doesn't really like camping. Besides, sometimes, it's best that we spend time apart." Then he added, almost as an afterthought, "Michael, if you ever decide to get married, and I'm sure that's the last thing on your mind right now, but if and when you ever do, make sure that you know that person, and that she knows you. Don't keep anything from her, and make sure that she doesn't keep anything from you. Just remember that." With that he fell silent, and never mentioned the subject again. For a short while, he wondered what had brought such a notion on, but soon forgot about it himself, and put in it the far reaches of his memory. Now, with Jane's words, it came bursting to the surface, flooding his thoughts.

She could tell that he was absorbing these secrets, and sat quietly waiting for him to finish. When he spoke again, he said to her, "You know, I didn't even know who you were an hour ago, and now it seems like you know more about my family than I do. It's weird, real weird." Then he asked, "Did David tell you what happened to the baby?"

"He said only that the child died young. I know nothing beyond that."

"Oh. "He looked at her. "Funny that I never heard anything about this over the years, not even a trace of a rumor. It must have been kept real quiet. And it obviously affected David, and I'm sure my sister Susan too."

She nodded and continued her remembrances. "David felt as if he was witness to a great crime, not just your mother cheating on your father, but also your father. According to him, your father was also partly to blame; he was rarely at home, working and going to school so much. Basically, he neglected your mother. He saw it as both their faults, and got turned off to the whole marriage thing."

"Were you and David ever married?"

"No, we never got officially married. But we committed ourselves to each other."

"Well, what did you two do all those years?"

"At first, we wandered a lot. We wanted to see the country, to try to find a place that suited us best, where we felt comfortable. After the commune, we lived in Cleveland for a while, and worked in restaurants. Then we were in Milwaukee for a couple of years. I worked in a department store and David in a sporting goods outlet. There were a couple of other places, I don't remember all of them. I think one of the best towns was St. Paul, Minnesota. Even though he didn't have a college degree, David got a job as a math teacher at a small private school, and I was a teacher's aide in another school. We had summers off, and used to go canoe camping at the border lakes. You know where those are?" and he nodded. "We moved around for about ten years, and really didn't settle down until the kids were born."

He sat up. "So you did have children. I heard stories that David fathered four or five children."

She looked at him and shook her head. "No, those stories are wrong. Only two. A girl and a boy. Martha and Jason. We didn't have children until we were in our thirties. We wanted to experience life first, and so we did."

He looked at her. "Where are they now?"

"Martha lives not too far from here. She's married, has one child."

"And Jason? The boy?"

She turned as dark as she had been when he first saw her at the door. "He joined the Army out of high school, and was sent to Afghanistan about a year after 9-11. Was killed on patrol in 2003." She said it without emotion, and then quickly went on. "That was one of the few things that David and I argued about. Letting him join up for the military. You see, we were very anti-military when we were in college.

94

Then ironically, our son wants to sign up. David wouldn't let him, I didn't like it either, but I said he had to make up his own mind, he was an adult, we couldn't tell him what to do. He wanted to serve, then go to school on the GI Bill. That's how he had it figured. Something got in the way, though, and he came home in a box. Sacrificed himself to save three other soldiers who were under fire. Won the Silver Star for bravery. I have it in a drawer in the bedroom. Of course, it doesn't make a lot of difference to him anymore." She concluded. "I should have never let him enlist. Funny how things are always clear afterwards."

He changed the conversation. "You know, in all this talk, I never asked you where David is now. I assume you know where he is."

She said, "Of course. He's right here."

"Where?"

She got up and left the room for a minute. He assumed that she was in a back bedroom. He could hear a closet door opening and closing. Then she came out carrying a small white porcelain vase with a tight lid on the top. "He's here. This is your brother."

He looked at the vase. "He died?"

"About a year ago. Last March, to be exact. Heart attack. He had been having heart problems for a couple of years. Didn't tell me about them, but I knew. He would rub his chest on occasion, and sometimes give a little gasp of pain, and then just shrug it off to coming old age. I kept telling him to go to the doctor, but he wouldn't. Then one day he was out walking and had a heart attack. Some people tried to help him and he was taken to a hospital, but it was too late. I got a call from the hospital, and that was all. No service, no memorial, nothing in the paper. It was the way David wanted it. He told me years ago that he didn't want a big deal made about his death. He said, 'People live their lives and then they're gone. That's all.' I'd prefer to remember him as he was alive, and now that he's dead, the memories are good enough for me. I've kept his ashes, though." She stopped for a moment, as if she was trying to decide something. "Now that you're here, though, would you want to have them? He mentioned you quite a bit over the years, and told me once that he'd wished that he could have gotten to know you better." She offered him the vase.

He thought about it for a minute, then replied, "No, you were closest to him for most of his life. I really hardly knew him, much as it would bring some kind of closure to me. Well, in a way, being here has brought closure. That's enough." He gave the vase back to her, and she put it up on a book shelf.

Then she sat back down in the chair. "I've talked most of the time so far. Now, what about your life?"

As he had done so many times on this trip, he talked about his life and his job in California, his marriage and the two girls, and Beatrice's death, and how he decided to take a trip. When he mentioned that Beatrice had died almost a year before in March as well, she smiled and commented, "Strange coincidence." He mentioned a few of the people he had met, and the impression that some of them had made on him, while others had been left behind without a thought. Most of all, he talked about how he had loved Beatrice, even though she sometimes became exasperated with his seemingly logical and straightforward approach to life. But he reminded himself that she had been with him for almost thirty years, and as he did so, he realized that Jane and David had been a pair for over thirty years as well, and thought of the parallel lives they had led, and how happy and content they had all been. And as he finished, he smiled to himself.

By this time, it was afternoon, and he realized that he had taken up too much of Jane's time. He assumed that she would have to go to work, or have some other appointment, but she seemed in no hurry for him to leave. When he apologized for barging in on her, she smiled and said, "No, not at all. This is my day off. I don't work again until Friday. In some ways, it's been wonderful meeting you. As I mentioned before, David told me about you, and how he hoped that you would grow up to be upright and successful, and it sounds like you have. I'm glad you took the time to find him."

He asked her one question as he prepared to leave. "Do you think I could meet Martha, and at least get to know her a little bit? After all, she's a part of my family as well."

"I'll call her tonight, and tell her about you. She knows only that her father had family, that's all. But I think she'd like to see you." He gave her his cell phone number and email address, and told her, "I'll be here for a while more. Get in touch with me when you hear something." And, after shaking her hand, he left.

In a phone call the next day, Jane told him that Martha wanted to meet him. "She was a bit apprehensive at first," she said, "but then she came around, and is now looking forward to meeting you. She's met relatives on my side, but you know about David's not connecting. She's really kind of excited about it."

"How old is she now?" he asked.

Jane thought for a minute on the phone. "She'll be thirty-three this August. She came first, and then Jason was born three years later." She gave him the directions to a downtown restaurant and told him to be there at noon the following day.

He walked in the door, told that hostess he was looking for someone, then saw them in a table near the corner. Or, he saw Jane first. Then he stopped and stared for a minute. The young woman seated next to her was his daughter Laura. Or rather her double. The same facial shape, the same lips, the same eyes and nose. Even the same basic hair style. He stood there taking in her family resemblance, of how much she was a member of the Lindstrom clan. And the boy sitting by her could have been the spitting image of his father, Stephen Lindstrom, the man from the Minnesota Great Plains. He wondered at how marvelous it was, the family lineage and the power of genes and memory.

Finally, he continued on his way to the table and stopped in front of it. Jane, wearing worn but clean clothes, stood up and shook his hand. Then she turned to the young woman, her daughter, and said, "Martha, I'd like you to meet your uncle, Michael Lindstrom. Michael, this is Martha, and her son Stephen." Jane was much more animated and relaxed than she had been two days before.

He shook hands all around, and especially took the boy's hand. "I almost can't believe it, "He said. "It's like finding lost treasure years after giving up looking for it." They all laughed and he sat down in the remaining chair. He turned to Martha and told her, "I apologize for staring at you like that. You look so much like my daughter Laura." And he pulled out his iPhone and scrolled to her image. Martha looked at it for a minute, and then blurted out with "Oh, wow. It's like I'm looking at myself in the mirror. You say this is Laura. How old is she? And do you have any other children?"

"Laura is twenty-six. And yes, I have another daughter, Danae, who's twenty-one and in college." He spoke easily now, after all, he was among family. He looked at the little boy. "And Stephen, you look so much like your great-grandfather, my father. And his name was Stephen as well. I just came from where he grew up, in Minnesota."

Now the conversation was flowing freely, and Martha asked him about his life, and where he had been on his trip, and about Beatrice; Jane had obviously clued her concerning her death, and he answered all her questions while they ordered their food and then ate. Again, he was afraid that he would be using up their time, but they seemed to be not concerned with it, kept talking well into the afternoon, as if they wanted to know everything about him; after all, Jane had almost forty years to catch up on, and Martha a few less, and he, too, wanted to learn who they were and their experiences. Martha, he found out, had been born in St. Paul, but then grew up in Buffalo and attended SUNY, majoring in business. Currently, she was an accountant who had her own business. Unlike her parents, she had married, to a man now a bank manager, whom she had originally met in college.

He told Martha about his marriage and her aunt Beatrice, and their life and love together, and her experience with cancer. He tried to keep a straight face as he mentioned it, but at times he lost his composure and tears leaked out of his eyes. She expressed her sympathies, and he wished that Beatrice could have met this young woman who looked so much like her daughter, and, indeed, was so much like her in many other ways as well.

During the afternoon, he talked more with Jane, and learned about her background. She was the youngest of four. Her father served in the Army in World War II, and came home afterwards to be an insurance agent, but stayed in the reserves. "He was called up for active duty in 1951, and sent to Korea. He was killed five months later. I was only about three at the time, so I really don't remember him." Her mother never got over it, and ended up in a mental hospital, and she and her two brothers and sister lived with their grandparents. "I was more or less on my own from about thirteen on," she told him. "My grandfather died when I was ten, and then my grandmother got sick a lot, and I took care of her, and tried to go to school as well. She died when I was sixteen, and then I moved in with my oldest brother until I went to college. That's probably why I was attracted to David. He had a really disrupted family life, too. We kind of found comfort in each other." He asked her about her job. "Oh, I work at the JC Penny here as a sales clerk. I like it. I enjoy working with people. I would go crazy if I had a factory job where I did the same thing every day. David liked to work with people also. He was really good at it."

"What did David do all the time you lived in Buffalo?"

"He worked in a bookstore. Started off as a sales clerk, and eventually became the head manager. He liked it; even though he never finished college, he was always reading and learning; he more or less taught himself business and finance, and he liked to meet and talk to the people who came in. He ended up being good at management, too. He had some offers from other companies in the Buffalo area, but the owners kept talking him into staying. He was there for almost thirty years. He found his niche there."

"Then why did he work in a little storefront restaurant the last few years of his life?"

Jane thought for a moment, then replied. "He just wanted something to do two or three days a week, and it went back to when he and I worked in restaurants when we were young. And he liked that place as well. Small, comfortable, friendly people. By that time, it was just the two of us, and we didn't need much money. We've never had that much, and we've somehow always gotten along."

"How did you end up in Buffalo?"

She smiled. "You make it sound like it's the worst place on Earth. Sort of like what I've heard about Fresno." He smiled back at her, and she went on. "Actually, it's pretty nice here during the summer and fall. The winters are what get people down. We decided to visit Niagara Falls one year; we had a friend from Mizzou who moved here after graduation. We really liked the area and ended up staying. Martha was about a year old at the time."

He also asked her about Susan. "I've talked to her on the phone and met her a few times, but I really don't know her that well. Martha met her once or twice, too, when she was growing up." Martha nodded in agreement. "But she was always very distant, hard to get to know and get close to. That's always been my impression of her. David told me some things about her, how her life was kind of messed up because of what happened with your folks, or at least that was his story. She and David would write letters to each other a lot. She knew about us and where we were living and what we were doing, but I guess she never said anything about it to your parents. It was like she and David had some kind of secret agreement, that they were protecting each other."

When it came time to leave, he was genuinely grateful that he had the opportunity to meet all of them. He gave Jane a big hug, which they had not done before, and he invited Martha and Stephen to visit California in the future. He could hardly wait for Laura and Danae to see their cousin, and he, too, felt, relieved that he had at least partially solved a family mystery, one that had been on his conscience, and its revelation made more room for his feelings about Beatrice. In a way, the finding of part of his family had melted away some of the agony for him. He still missed her, but the inclusion of new members was making up for it.

That night, when he sat down to write in his journal, he found the words hard to form. The feelings, the emotions of meeting a branch of his family for the first time were almost too much to handle; he was overwhelmed with warmth and gratefulness. Finally, he simply wrote, "Met David's partner and daughter and her son. And glad I did. If nothing else important happens on this trip, it will have all been worth it."

March

As he drove east he could see the beginnings of spring. The sun was higher in the sky as well, and he knew that in a few months summer would burst out in an explosion of light and heat. In the meantime, he thought of what he would say to his sister. Her visits to St. Louis after she married were rare, and when he and his parents moved to California, almost non-existent. He had not seen her in person since their father's funeral in Swensen, and she attended it only because she was living in nearby Madison, Wisconsin, at the time. Several years afterwards, when he determined that their mother could no longer take care of herself and he proposed moving her from Sacramento to an assisted living facility in Fresno, she replied brusquely on the phone, "You take care of it. Do whatever." Three years later, he called to tell her of their mother's death, she said she would come, but never did, and later wrote to say that she just didn't feel well enough to travel. Now that he knew, or thought he knew, about what had happened when she was a child, some of her behavior was explained, but for him there were still blanks in her life.

He had called Susan from Buffalo and told her about meeting Jane Andrews and the knowledge of his nephew and niece. She did not sound surprised, and did not appear to be particularly happy about him visiting, but she didn't say no either. Her ambivalence puzzled him. He would have to wait until they met and talked over what he had learned.

As a historian, he thought about driving to Boston. Boston was where the American Republic had begun, the Boston Tea Party, the Battle of Bunker Hill, the home of Adams, the birthplace of Franklin, the origin of many other founders. At the same time, he thought about Beatrice again. He had not done much of that in recent weeks as the revelations of his family consumed him. He knew people who had lost their spouses and they hardly went out to meet others, or rarely went outside at all. Others were out partying and dancing only a week or two after the services. He thought of Jane, and wondered if she did anything other than work. From observing her apartment, he got the idea that she didn't leave often other than to go to work. The ways we deal with death, he reflected.

He stopped in Lynn, on the outskirts of Boston, where Susan lived. Despite the evidence of the new season, the temperature was still cold, and snow was still piled up in places, reminders that winter held on, dominating the land and the sky, no matter what people thought. In California, kids would be wearing their shorts and tank tops to school, explaining that, "Spring will be here soon," and at the same time trying not to show how cold they were. Here it was still in the forties during the day and down to the teens at night. The students he saw were wearing long pants, long sleeved shirts, and winter jackets. They knew better than their West Coast counterparts.

He spent a few days by himself, visiting the Boston Commons, Braintree, The Old North Church, and other now touristy sights. One day on a whim, he drove out to Cape Cod and all the way up the spit to Provincetown, where, on a grey and formidable afternoon, he watched the Atlantic slam up against the jetty, and felt the sting of the sea water as it hit his face. A storm was coming in, he concluded. He thought of himself and Beatrice coming to this place once many years ago, shortly after they were married and before the girls came along and, despite the weather, how much they enjoyed it. He could still see Beatrice looking far out into the Atlantic, to the horizon, as if she thought she could see all the way to Europe.

Eventually, though, he would meet with Susan, and after several days he called her and they made plans to meet at a local restaurant. He wondered why all personal encounters took place in restaurants. Maybe because it had to deal with food, he thought. Everything ultimately revolves around food, the basic staple of life.

He was there at the appointed time. He waited in the foyer until Susan came in, and when he saw her, he rose and greeted her, not with a hug, but a handshake and a smile. He had not seen her in almost fifteen years; she had put on weight, but still looked good, and her hair was no longer below her shoulders, but a pageboy crop, brown and grey. Her face had new lines about it, and her eyes could only be said to be sad and troubled. She was someone who was under a good deal of pressure and stress, he thought. Whether she would give the reasons for it at this meeting, he would see. He could tell that she in turn was examining him.

"How are Diana and Matthew?" he asked her. Like her, he had not seen her children in many years either, and wondered what their lives were like.

"They're fine," she replied, and left it at that. He decided not to take offense, and would wait until later.

The hostess came and led them to a table for two. He ordered an ice tea, and she a diet cola. Then they sat back and faced each other. What had happened to make things come to this, he wondered, what went out of kilter with our lives so long ago, that we see each other only in places like this, in almost forced encounters that neither of us really wants, but are necessary for survival.

She broke his musing by saying, "Michael, I know it's perhaps too late, but I'm sorry I couldn't make it to Beatrice's funeral. I know it was over a year ago. But I'm really sorry. It must have been hard on you."

He replied, "It was, but I'm thankful for Laura and Danae. They got me through everything, and made it, well, somewhat easier."

She looked at him intently for a second, and then said, "You've changed, changed a lot. Granted, it's been several years, but you're not the same brother that I knew once."

"Susan, I think that most of the change has been in the last year or so. Ever since Beatrice's death. I've come to realize how much life is still ahead of me. To be honest, Beatrice was my world, but, and I've been thinking about this a lot lately, I'm learning to go on without her. Maybe all the traveling has given me a wider perspective on life. And I think that Beatrice would have wanted me to be this way. I guess, to put it simply, life goes on, and you do the best you can." Then he looked at his sister hard, trying to see through the mask of her face and eyes and into her spirit. He decided to be direct. "Susan, what's been happening to you? Why has there always been so much distance between us? And what do you know about David? When I talked to Jane Andrews in Buffalo, what she told me blew me away. I found it hard to believe. What do you know about all this?"

Susan held up her hands, and then shook her head, causing her hair to fly off on trajectories of its own. She sat for a moment, then began to answer. "It's not you, Michael, it really isn't. I've made a mess of my life. The reason I didn't come to the services was because I had just broken up with my husband. We were starting divorce proceedings right around then. I was going through so much, but I just couldn't face you with my situation dragging along. So I decided not to come." She was on the verge of crying, and Michael offered his napkin, but she waved it away.

"I'm sorry to hear that. So you're single again?" She nodded. "Are you doing all right financially? I can help you if you need it."

She shook her head negatively. "No, really, I'm okay. My job actually pays pretty well. I'm union, I get good benefits and regular raises. That's not the problem."

"Have you ever gotten counseling?"

"I'm in counseling right now. I see a therapist once a week. This has been for over a year now, ever since, Kyle, number three, and I split up. And actually, we were in marriage counseling before that. Like I was in marriage counseling with Jeff, and in marriage counseling with William. For all the good it all did." She turned away from him as if to hide her disgust with herself.

The waiter came to take their order, and after he left she continued. "I don't know where to start, Michael. You were too young to understand everything that was going on when David and I were growing up. And you don't really know about what happened before you were born. Let me put it this way: did you ever wonder why you were born so long after me and David?"

He studied her and shrugged. "Well, I never thought seriously about it. Lots of people have babies spaced years apart. I had this student, a sophomore girl, in my history class several years ago whose mother had a baby when she, the girl, was sixteen. It happens, probably more often than most people think. Or maybe my birth was, as they say, an 'accident.' Mom and Dad were human; they may have just gotten carried away one night later in life. I've read that people can't imagine their parents having sex, but it has to have happened; otherwise we wouldn't be here."

He was both surprised and also pleased when Susan laughed, and he had to smile along with her. "Michael, thanks. That kind of makes me feel a little bit better. But that's not exactly what happened. Exactly what was it that Jane told you?"

He recounted the conversation in Buffalo from a month earlier, and Susan listened carefully. When he finished, she said nothing, but sat back and closed her eyes. Then she opened them. "Basically, that's correct, but she left some things out. Maybe she didn't want to hurt you even more, or maybe David didn't tell her everything. First of all, yes, I've known for a long time where David was and what he was doing. We kept in touch over the years. I also saw him every once in a while. We kind of had an unspoken agreement not to say much about our whereabouts. David in particular. He just didn't want anyone to know where he was or what he was doing. As he got older, I'm not sure why. But that was up to him. When Jane called me to say that he had died, I cried, but was also relieved. I was planning to write and tell you, but then your wife died, number three and I broke up, and the whole world was going to hell. And I just let it go. You can understand that, can't you?"

He nodded to say he did, and she went on. "It's true that mom had an affair and got pregnant. This was when I was about two. David was around five. Mom made a mistake. There's no other way to put it. Dad was working day in and day out to keep us going, and also going to school so much he was hardly at home, and I guess she got bored and felt she needed more than a small apartment and two children. From what I know, she met this guy at the grocery store, they started seeing each other, and, well, had an affair. They would meet while Dad was at work or when Dad was at home taking care of us, and Mom told him she had to 'go shopping' or something like that. I don't remember it, but David told me once that he would come over at times while Dad was

103

gone. I never knew the man's name, and I don't think David did either; later on, we would just call him 'mom's friend.' Dad eventually found out, again, how, I don't know. She and Dad separated, and she went to live with this guy. I never knew his name or much about him. About a month later, mom found out she was pregnant by him. Mom had the baby, but then it died only a few days after birth; it was a girl, and apparently she had some kind of disability or congenital defect. I don't think she was even given a name. After that, Mom and the guy broke up. From what I heard, the guy blamed Mom for the baby's death and left her, and then Mom thought she would just waltz back into Dad's life as if nothing ever happened."

"Where were you and David all this time?" he asked.

"We were shuttled back and forth between dad and mom. Dad insisted that he could take care of us, but, Mom got us most of the time. So, for about six or seven years we lived in a grungy, and I mean grungy, apartment above a garage in downtown St. Louis while Mom worked, and we had Mom's family as babysitters."

He was going to ask something, but stopped for a minute, and then remembered his maternal grandmother. She died when he was only about nine years old, but delving deeply, he imaged a stern old woman, gray hair, iron eyes, full of temper, ready to lash out at everyone and everything. Even at that young age, he and his cousins, especially Denise, who was only six at the time, were terrified of her and stayed away from her. It was in those young years that they began their filial bond that continued to the present. Why was his grandmother always so mad, he pondered, thinking about it for the first time in almost forty years.

As if she was reading his mind, Susan answered his question. "Do you remember how Grandma used to always be on everyone's case, especially ours? I think it was because of the way that Mom turned out. She was angry at Mom, for, well, being what she saw as unfaithful, for running out on Dad, and then having a baby out of wedlock. Michael, today, people think nothing of that, but in those days, the early '50s, it was almost unheard of. Women who had children outside of marriage were called sluts, whores, ostracized almost everywhere. Mom was lucky to get a job, and it barely kept us going."

But then she stopped talking for a minute and reflected. The she continued. "But Dad was kind of responsible as well. He was hardly ever at home. Between work and school and all of his other activities, he basically ignored Mom. I mean, Dad didn't realize that she needed him at home, and he wasn't, at least when he should have been. Michael, if I've learned anything from my marriages, a separation or divorce is

104

rarely only one person's fault. Both are involved in some way. Dad was essentially a good person, and I know you pretty much idolized him; Mom was, in her own way, a good person, too. But at that time, and in that situation, they both made mistakes."

Susan stopped, and drew into herself, disappearing from the present, and then she came back and continued. "Mom, I guess, just wasn't grown up enough when they got married. The only thing I can assume is that she just wasn't ready to settle down, she was only about eighteen or nineteen, and should have waited a few more years. She and Dad got hitched right after the war, he was the returning soldier-hero, and I guess that when he proposed, she couldn't say no." She stopped talking for a minute, and then continued. "I don't know. For a long time, I blamed Mom for everything that happened and what David and I experienced, and I was real angry at her. But maybe as I've gotten older, and especially in the last few years, I've come to the conclusion that it was both their faults, and it really wasn't either one's fault. Things like that just happen. Does that make sense?"

He looked at his sister and thought of what she and his brother went through during the years that their parents were apart. How the experience forged an animosity between the generations, and why they wanted to get away. But there was a piece missing.

"If what you say is all valid, and I believe you, then where do I come in?" he asked her.

"Michael, I don't know all the details, probably never will, but mom and dad still kind of loved each other, there was still something there, don't ask me how or why. Even though they were separated, they would meet every now and then, I mean, not when David and I went back and forth between them, but on their own, and I guess they kind of rekindled what they once had. I think that Mom, once she was a bit older, really regretted what she had done, how immature she had been, how much she had hurt Dad and messed up their lives. And, Dad, well, I think that by then Dad had more free time and understood that he need to be more involved and more helpful as well, and was willing to let things move on. Anyway, after being apart for six-seven years, they decided to give it a try again, and moved back in together, and about two years later you came along. That's essentially what happened. By then, it was too late for David and me. But you had a chance to have a normal life, and Mom, and particularly Dad, tried hard to make sure that you did. I guess you can put it this way: they were both in their late twenties, early thirties by then, wiser, more mature. Mom, I guess, was more settled, more responsible. And by then, Dad was older too and had a steady good paying job and could spend more time with Mom and us.

105

And so they lived, not always happily, but forever after, if you want to put it that way."

"No more problems, huh? Just like that?"

"Well, Mom almost slipped once. From what I heard, and I was told this years later by Aunt Peggy, she started getting interested in a guy she knew at work. Dad found out about it, and that's how you moved to California."

He nodded. "I thought we moved because dad got a job offer there."

Susan agreed with him. "Apparently Dad had had the offer for some time. He never accused mom or anything, but he decided that that was the time to take it and leave. And I guess it was a way out for Dad. I don't think he ever really liked St. Louis. He and Mom's parents and sister never quite got straightened out. I mean, they never argued or anything like that, but they just never saw eye to eye. And the city just wasn't his type of place. He probably would have preferred to go back to Minnesota."

By this time, their food had come, and they ate quietly over the ambient noise of the dining room. Funny, he thought, how intimate a place like this can be, even with strangers all around you. He looked around and wondered how many of them had family stories, hidden filial mysteries that needed time to be released to the right people.

After several minutes of silent dining, he spoke again. "Susan, you sound like you're the one who holds all the family secrets." He looked at her with a smile. "Is that why you've made yourself so off limits all these years?"

"No, a few other people are aware of what happened. I don't know about Dad's family. Dad's funeral was the first time I'd seen them in probably twenty years, and I haven't heard from any of them since. But Aunt Peggy knows. I've always been closer to Mom's side than Dad's. Aunt Peggy took care of us a lot when Mom and Dad were separated and Mom was working. After my first divorce, I went to St. Louis a couple of times to see her, and she told me a lot about Mom and Dad. She knows the whole story."

"Aunt Peggy is in a care facility in Columbia. Denise and I saw her at Christmas. She has dementia and it's getting worse; I doubt if she'd still remember anything. She didn't even know who I was." He sat back in his chair. "The older generation is passing away, and we'll be the elders. You know, thirty, forty years ago, I never thought that would happen. And here we are now."

Susan smiled at him. "Wait until you have grandchildren, then you'll really feel old. I know."

"How's that?"

She grinned, "Michael, I'm a grandmother five times over now. Diana has twin girls ten years old, and a boy six, and Matthew has two little boys. I'm way ahead of you. Speaking of which, how are your girls doing?"

He told her about Danae and Laura, glad to move away from the storm and into something more pleasant. When he finished, he could tell that she felt lighter. "They've never really met their cousins on the East Coast," she said. "You'll have to bring them here someday. They'd like this part of the country."

He shrugged and held up his hands. "They have lives of their own now, and their own way of doing things. I'll talk to them though."

The dinner was finished, the dishes were cleared, and the check was presented. They split it after a short debate.

As they were leaving, he said, "You still haven't said anything about David. When do I get to learn that?"

Susan thought for a minute, looked at her watch, then replied, "Thursday, about six, come over to my place. I'll give you directions to it. I'll cook something and we'll go over David. Now that you know about the family, you might as well know everything about the family."

During the week, he thought back and tried to bring memories of his parents to the surface. He and his father had gone fishing, camping, backpacking together. His father showed him how to pour and finish cement, how to build a cabinet, how to fix a car engine and reline brakes. He remembered his father teaching him to drive. "Now put your left foot on the clutch pedal, push it all the way down, and shift. Then let up slowly on the clutch and give some gas with your right foot. That's it. Little by little...," as the car jerked forward in the deserted college parking lot on Sunday afternoons. His father was patient with him, rarely getting angry, but clearly expressing disappointment when he brought home less than expected grades from school, or goofed off on the baseball field during summer Little League games. There was a time for fun, his father's voice and eyes said, but there is also a time for seriousness, and the mark of a successful person is knowing when to separate the two. And from this spare, unassuming man, he slowly learned to face the world and find his way in it.

Of his mother, even though she had died more recently, his recollections of her were much dimmer. She had been an office assistant and then secretary for many years. He knew her as a quiet and thoughtful, almost dreamy, person, who often went off on her own without any forewarning or notice. There was a wooded area behind the house in Webster Groves, and sometimes on Saturdays or Sundays he and his father would come home from a ball game or church and find her gone, and a note on the kitchen counter saying, "I'll be back in a little while." Eventually, he would see her coming out of the woods with a book or a magazine, and he knew that she had spent the afternoon reading next to the creek that ran through the woods. Occasionally, at night, he would hear the back door open, and looking down from his second story bedroom window, he would see her looking up at the sky, as if inviting the stars to come down to Earth and make conversation with her. She did not scold or yell at him, but she also seemed to keep a distance from him, especially after he became a teen. As to her relationship with his father, he would see them talking quietly at times using words that were intended for them only, and they would sometimes pat each other on the back or shoulder, but otherwise, his mother was kind of an enigma to him, and he realized many years later that he knew very little about her.

On Thursday, he was at Susan's apartment, a modest two bedroom affair in a complex on the outskirts of Lynn. When she opened the door, she did not take his hand, but gave him a hug, and asked him to come in. The place was older; he estimated it had been built in the 1960s, but clean and well decorated. In the living room, there was a trace of the Susan he had once known: the sophisticated and articulate young woman who had a universal interest in art, music, literature, culture. He remembered when, as a seventeen-year old, she made all county youth honor orchestra on the oboe, and wondered if she still played it. He noticed the copies of Dali prints on the wall. Her stereo cabinet held compositions by Beethoven, Stravinsky, Mahler, Copland, and Handel. On top of the bookcase was a number of ceramic animals and birds; he picked up a small porcelain owl and looked at it. The shelves underneath were full of best sellers, past and present; as he glanced through the titles, he noticed, almost to his surprise, that all three of Beatrice's novels were in it. He pulled one out and examined it, her first work, *The River's Flow,* by Beatrice Cardoso. He recalled the time that she started writing it, shortly after Danae was born, and she was taking a maternity sabbatical: the months of late nights typing, the seemingly endless revisions, the uncountable times she announced, "I'm finished," then more revisions, and finally, the day that the letter came saying that a publisher had accepted it. A long hard journey. It sold well, as did her subsequent two, and he proudly took her out to dinner the day that each came out in print. He was perusing it when Susan came into the room.

She noticed what he had in his hand, and came over to his side.

"You know, for a long time I was envious of Beatrice. I met her only a few times, but she seemed so perfect, she was everything that I had hoped to be: educated, intelligent, successful. She was also the kind of spouse that I would want to have had. You two were married for almost, what, thirty years, and I think of the disasters my marriages have been in comparison." She looked at a distant wall. "At times, I wish I had stayed at Bryn Mawr. How different things might have been."

He put his arm around her. "Sis, we just did the best we could, no secret plan, no magic formula, no great achievements or fireworks. We had our ups and downs as well. Somehow we worked out everything and managed to stay together. I will say that the last couple of years were hard, but we had years of capital built up and got through them. Even towards the end, Beatrice was apologizing to me for putting me though all this. I told her, 'Not to worry, this is what I'm here for,' although I sometimes feel that I could have done more for her. I think that, in a way, I'll always be married to her. Speaking of Bryn Mawr, did you ever think of going back to school?"

She shook her head sadly. "I tried once or twice, taking classes at a couple of different junior colleges. But something always got in the way. My husbands, my problem," by which he assumed she meant her drinking, "the kids, a lot of things. I know those are all excuses, but I just never saw it through. Maybe when I retire, I'll have the time and motivation to finally be serious about it."

He put the book back on the shelf and picked up a *National Geographic* that was laying in the coffee table, noticing that it was that month's issue. He complemented her on her tastes in art and design, then they sat and talked about trivia in the kitchen while she worked at the stove, boiling pasta, cooking vegetables, and stirring alfredo sauce. The room was full of savory smells and sounds while she questioned him about his teaching job, his travels across the country, and his life in general. He told her as much as he deemed possible, and left it at that. He was sure that she would have done the same.

When they sat down to eat, he learned that Susan was, in fact, a good cook. He enjoyed the meal, and the fresh home-made bread that went with it. They ate for a few minutes in silence, after which Susan busied herself going over to the stove and then the refrigerator. When she opened the door, he felt a breeze of coldness flow through the room. Then she returned, and they resumed.

Finally, he asked about their brother and she stopped eating for a minute, wordlessly took a piece of bread, broke it and ate. She looked away, then looked at him, and decided to speak. When it came, it was with a tone of both sorrow and sadness. He had the idea that she could not speak in any other way concerning herself and David.

"Michael, you need to understand that what David did and how he lived his life was his own choice. I didn't influence him, nor did anyone else really. Well, maybe Jane. I'll tell you what I know. After what he and I saw of our parents and what happened to them, he decided to start fresh and anew. He wanted to get as far away from everyone as he could, and he did. Except for me. He and I were kind of bound to each other; the only way I can put it is that we suffered together and survived together. It was kind of an unspoken mutual agreement that we would be each other's confidant when the rest of the family was gone. And that's the way we lived. When he went off to college, he had already decided to get away; he and I had talked about it on many occasions when he was in high school. I was to follow him and we would disappear into our own lives away from everyone else. So we more or less did."

"Did you always know where he was?" he asked.

"Pretty much so. We wrote letters to each other, not all the time, but enough. When he and Jane moved around, he would send me his address and phone number. He called me when his children were born and at important times in their lives. He was a good father, and he and Jane tried to be good parents. Maybe it was because of what happened to Mom and Dad."

He nodded, "And maybe also what happened to Jane," and told her of what Jane had said about her early life. Susan listened quietly, and when he finished said, "I never knew any of that about her, David never said anything about it. Interesting."

She continued. "I would see him once a year, or maybe every other year. We would meet and talk, kind of the way you and I are right now. It was always at a restaurant or a diner or someplace like that. He didn't want to meet any of my husbands, he was afraid that they would talk when and if we ever met a relative. I watched him as he grew older over the years. When his son was killed was when he really started to age. I think that's when his heart problems began as well; from then on it was kind of downhill for him."

"Jane has his ashes in an urn. She tried to give them to me. I'm not sure if I would know what to do with them."

Susan closed her eyes and then opened them again. "Michael, gathering from what he told me, David really loved you and the only regret he had in leaving the family was that he wouldn't be able to see you grow up. I would tell him how you were doing, your job, your marriage, your children, and I'm sure it was the kind of life he always wanted to have. But he just couldn't bring himself to reach out and

110

return to the fold. He had that sense of dignity and pride that Dad had, of sticking with something no matter what the consequences. And in that way, he admired and respected Dad. I do know this: maybe about two or three years after Dad died, David made a trip to Minnesota, he told me this, and he went to Swensen and visited Dad's grave, and all the places that he remembered about the family when he was young, before everything happened that caused Mom and Dad to split up. I think that was the closest he ever came to returning. He told me this one night when we were together. I get the idea that later in his life he came to realize that he had made a mistake, but it was too late to turn back, too late to try to undo everything. He felt that he had to just accept things for what they were. And that's what he did."

"Well," he said, "He had his own family by then. That must have been a comfort to him."

"Yes, but not in the same way. The last time I saw him was about two years ago. Jane called me and told me he wasn't doing well, and I drove to Buffalo to see him. We talked for quite a while, and he told me that eventually he'd want people to know where he was and what happened to him. He felt he'd been a failure in life, not in being a father or a brother, but just as a human being in general, that he could have done more and contributed more, and maybe he'd be redeemed by people knowing about him. Well, he got better after that, but then several months later he had a heart attack and that was it." She held back the tears. "He really was a good person, you know. I think that if you had been around him more and gotten to know him, you'd agree."

He nodded and replied, "From what Jane told me, he did very well, doing what he wanted to do, working in the bookstore, raising the children. I'm impressed with Martha. She seems to have a good head on her shoulders. He can't call himself a failure after raising a child like her.

Do you have any pictures of him, anything that was taken over the years?"

"I don't, no. Jane might. They lived very simply, so I'm not sure if they even had a camera. But I do have something else that you can have before you leave Boston."

"Susan," he suddenly asked, "How are you doing? How is your health?"

She sat up in her chair and gave him a smile. "I can't say I've conquered my drinking, but I can control it now. A year ago, when all these things were coming at me, I almost lost it. I came real close to going back on the bottle, as they say. I haven't had any alcohol for almost five years. AA has helped quite a bit. I always thought it was for other people." She looked at him with pride, and he reached over and

111

grabbed and squeezed her hand.

She rose to get dessert, and he helped her clear the table and wash the dishes. Afterwards, she talked far into the night about her children and grandchildren, and showed him dozens of pictures, as if to forget the memories of what she had said earlier. He, too, appreciated the family talk of so much happiness after so much despair.

A week later, after he had visited Lexington and Concord and Walden Pond and Emerson's house and the famous bridge, she invited him over again, and he met his nephew and niece and their children. Again, they talked for many hours and shared stories; they wanted to know all about their cousins in the West that they had never seen. This time the warmth of the stove and the flames in the fireplace in the family room warmed him. It was while they were all talking that he decided he would do something, but said nothing and let the evening go on.

Sometime during the evening, after Susan's children and their families had left, he told his sister, "You said earlier that your marriages were disasters, but I see Diana and Matthew and their spouses and children, and they're good people. You did a fine job of raising them, and that's what you should be proud of. You have nothing at all to be ashamed of." And she looked at him in the face, then kissed him on the cheek. "Thank you, Michael, I appreciate it. I know I haven't done many good things in my life, but it's nice to hear that."

As he was leaving, Susan gave him a bulky manila folder sealed with wrapping tape and told him to keep it. That night he read the letters that David had written to her. His brother's life came alive to him, and he wished forever afterwards that he had met him one more time and shared a bit with him. He read these letters throughout the night, and the morning sun was in the sky by the time he finished and put them aside and fell asleep on the bed, exhausted and tear-stained.

He slept all that day, awaking only to have dinner and write another long entry in his journal, and the following morning, he sent an extended email to Laura and Danae, telling them who he had seen and what he had learned, and that there had been a change in his plans. The next morning he packed up the Toyota, wrote another letter to his sister, and then left Lynn, traveling west.

April

As he walked the streets of Philadelphia, he felt as if he was in a beginning.

These were the streets that Jefferson strolled while he was writing the Declaration of Independence and Adams argued with Franklin and Mason and Dickinson and Rutledge. These same avenues and alleyways generated the conversations and debates that Madison incorporated into the Constitution. American history, he knew was recent compared to the events of Europe and Asia; their history was counted in millennia, not centuries or decades. But he thought America's history was something special; flawed as it was, it still shone out on the world, and invited millions to seek a better way of life, free from the tired and timeless disputes of the Old World. And in this city, he concluded, was where it began, something new and momentous was designed and born. Where it would lead, they did not know, he did not know, those to come would not know. But still, it began.

On his first full day in Philadelphia, a cloudless day coming out of winter and sliding into spring, with the flowers throwing forth their blazing colors and the tree in melodies of green, he drove, and then walked to Independence Hall, a stately steeple-topped building surrounded by office complexes and blaring traffic. There, among groups of impatient schoolchildren and steadfast senior citizens, he toured the building, visited the room where John Hancock held sway over a contentious Congress, and then signed his name to a final document large enough so the "the king could read it without his glasses." As he walked through the room, an older man next to him remarked, "Kind of gives you a shiver, doesn't it?" and he nodded. In a hallway just outside was a glass case with the "original" Declaration of Independence. The docent explained that the Declaration in Washington D.C. was what was called the Formal Presentation Copy; this was the printed Working Copy that was agreed on and first read on July 4, 1776. He smiled. It depended on what the definition of the Declaration was to make it official.

He saw the Liberty Bell as well, and decided that it was not that imposing or impressive. Nevertheless, it was a part of history as well, symbolic, if nothing else. Afterwards, he walked around the building, through the line of people waiting to enter, surveyed the area, and wondered what it was like during that summer of 1776; who, passing by on the dusty streets knew what was happening inside that building? He could only wonder, and walked on. A few blocks down the street was a small cemetery, and he turned into it. Against a wall, on the far side, he found what he was looking for, the grave of Benjamin Franklin, the marker covered with coins. Again, he wondered, what were the odds that so many far-seeing people living at the same time in the same place could come together and create what they did. Many scholars, people far more accomplished than he, had said that America was an accident, that it should never have existed. He could believe that, but here it was regardless.

He spent the rest of the day walking around the downtown area of the city, taking in its flavor and smells, poking around corners and peering into alleyways. At lunch he had a Philly cheesesteak sandwich, and for dinner, he ate at a small local diner. Then, as the sun was dipping between the buildings, he left the area and returned to his hotel room some miles away.

He spent another day at Valley Forge, meandering around the semi-wooded area, savoring the silence and the serenity, traveling from one marked place to another. Here was Washington's winter quarters, here was where von Stuben and his lieutenants trained the men of the Continental Army. Here were their winter huts, log buildings with little warmth and fewer comforts. As he walked the fields of Valley Forge, he again wondered about America being an accident, created in a sliver of a window where it was not possible before, and would hardly be possible again. It was opened for a brief period and then shut, perhaps forever. By the time he left the area it was nightfall, and from the distant trees came the call of an owl. His ears pricked up, and he listened to its familiar sound, then he moved on.

Another afternoon, he crossed the river and visited Princeton, not just to see the famous university, but also to visit the Revolutionary War battle site. He found it in a quiet meadow just outside the town and wandered around, trying to imagine the furor that took place there. So many battle sites, he thought, now calm and quiet, reverberated with the sound of gun and cannon fire; men shouting; others screaming, then moaning, then dying. How much blood was underneath this field, he pondered. Enough to throw off an oppressive government and establish a new country.

Then one day he decided to visit the King of Prussia Mall, some twenty miles west of Philadelphia. He had heard about this vast shopping center, one of the largest in the U.S., for some years. He was not a shopper as such, and rarely went beyond stores such as Target and Kohls. Nevertheless, he drove out to King of Prussia one afternoon, had no difficulty finding the huge sprawling complex, and wandered through its myriad of stores and displays. Some of the vendors were familiar to him; others were unknown. Some caught his view as bordering on the prosaic or in some cases, the ridiculous. For several hours, he wandered between the levels, brushing past multitudes of determined or even dedicated shoppers, as if they all were in some vast buzzing beehive, each of them with a job to do to ensure the betterment of the colony. He amused himself by thinking that some sociologist or anthropologist would have a field day studying this strange cavern-like culture, then walking away and shaking his head at the absurdity of it all.

He had dinner at one of the food courts, and it was there that he heard melodies from strings and horns. He walked down a vast corridor, and, after turning a corner, saw about twenty musicians setting up and practicing their instruments, apparently for a public concert. Customers were already gathering and watching as the players settled into their folding chairs, music stands in front of them, preparing for the performance. He elected to stay for it. Before she became ill, Beatrice had been an amateur cellist, and had often played in a group similar to this at schools, community centers, assisted-care homes, and other venues.

The group was along the lines of a chamber orchestra, with violins, violas, cellos, oboes, clarinets, bassoons, and flutes. When the musicians were settled, a short balding man wearing a dark suit stepped up to the conductor's podium, tapped his wand, and the concert commenced. The musicians played a variety of Renaissance and Baroque pieces, heavy on Bach and Handel. He stood against a pillar and absorbed the sounds coming from the instruments. The setting itself was not conducive to music, as the notes echoed off the walls and the glass panes and the corners of the mall. Yet, the music reached into him and reminded him of the days when he had gone to the concerts given by Beatrice and her group. It gave him a feeling of memory and passion, of warmth beyond mere external heat. The sounds, particularly those from the violins, propelled him to a time of beauty and comfort. He became weightless again, and his cares seemed a distant fire.

After about forty minutes of music and applause, the conductor announced a short break, and he moved back, out of the way of the crowd. About thirty feet away a table offered soft drinks and cookies, and he moved towards it. As he was sipping his drink next to the table, one of the musicians came up. He remembered her as one of the violinists, an Asian woman, maybe in her forties or early fifties, sharply defined features, ebony hair threaded with grey strands, slim and dignified. He resolved to thank her on their performance, and approached her.

"I would like to commend you and your group for your playing. I haven't heard such good music in a long time."

She smiled at him. "Thank you. Are you a musician also?"

"No, I don't play any instrument, but I enjoy listening to music. My wife was a musician who was in a group similar to yours, and I went to many of their performances."

"What pieces do you like?"

"I enjoy Bach's *Brandenburg Concertos*, *The Four Seasons* by Vivaldi, and also the *Watermusic* by Handel, and a piece by Pachelbel; I don't remember the name but I like the melody." And he whistled a few bars, going badly off tune by the end.

She laughed and replied, "Canon and Fugue in D. It's one of my favorites. We'll play it in the second half. "She suddenly changed the subject. " Your accent isn't from around here. Where are you from?"

"California, near Fresno," he replied.

She commented in jest. "You came all the way from California to hear us play? Are we that good?"

He smiled. "No, I'm traveling right now. I'm here on the east coast for, well, both personal and family business. I wanted to see Philadelphia; I haven't been in this area in several years. I happened to remember the King of Prussia Mall and came over. I'm glad I stayed."

"Well, I'm glad you like our music." She suddenly turned around. "Excuse me, we're starting to get ready for the second half. Nice to have met you, Mr...?"

"Lindstrom, Michael Lindstrom."

"I'm Elaine Chang. Enjoy the rest of the concert." And she left to take her seat.

He did enjoy the rest of the performance. The group played the Pachelbel piece, also a composition by Telemann, and a prelude by Bach. When it was finished, he clapped heartily, and gave a donation to an assistant moving around the crowd with a box. He went back to the refreshment table and bought another drink, and was standing there when she approached, violin case and a small purse in one hand and a music stand and portfolio of sheet music in the other.

"Well, did the second half satisfy you?"

"It certainly did. As good as any professional symphony orchestra, maybe better. And I mean that."

She smiled. "Don't flatter us too much. We could blow it all next time."

"The only thing you need is a harpsichord."

"Actually, we have one. One of our group plays an electronic keyboard that can be programed to sound like a harpsichord. But he couldn't be here today."

116

He looked at what she was holding. "Can I help you carry some of that? You seem to have your hands full."

She looked at him and said in a half serious half mocking tone. "I don't know. After all, I hardly know you. How do I know that you just won't run off with them?"

"Tell you what," he replied. "I'll give you my driver's license as a deposit." He pulled out his wallet, rummaged through it, and showed her a glossy laminated card. "It's the only one I have. See." And he opened up the entire wallet and dumped its contents into his hand.

She burst out laughing. "Put it away. You look trustworthy." She looked at him more seriously. "Have you had dinner yet?"

He looked back at her. "Yes, but I could have a dessert or something like that."

She took him back to the food court, to a salad bar place, where she ordered a chicken salad and drink. He went next door to a pie shop and bought a piece of pie and an ice tea. They sat and ate and talked.

"Lindstrom is a Swedish name. I have Swedish friends. But you say you're from California."

"Long roundabout story. My family was originally from Minnesota. I was actually born in St. Louis, but my parents moved west when I was a teenager. That's how I ended up out there."

"What do you do there?"

"I'm a schoolteacher. I teach high school history."

"I'm on the opposite end. I teach elementary school music. The school year is still in session, but you're traveling. Are you playing truant, then?"

"I took a leave of absence. My principal expects me back in the fall. In fact, she sends me emails about it all the time. My daughters told me I have to return by June." He smiled and shrugged. "They laid down the law to me before I left."

"Let me ask you this, then. Why are you traveling?"

He told her about Beatrice, her illness, and her death. She listened quietly and intently, saying nothing. For him, it was getting easier to talk about their life and her death; the pain was being replaced by an acceptance. He took out his iPhone and showed her Beatrice's picture, and well as some of Laura and Danae. A few times, he came close to crying, but he finished the story clear-eyed and smiling. "She died peacefully. We were around her bed, and I was holding one hand, and Laura and Danae were holding the other. And then she was gone. That's all. There's not much more to say."

He looked up at her, and saw compassion and sadness in her eyes. "Thank you for telling me that. It must have been hard for you."

"It was for a while, but not so much now. That's part of what I've learned during my trip. I'm sorry if it upset you."

"No, that's all right. You see, I lost Nelson, my husband, four years ago. I never got to say goodbye to him. He was at a business meeting one day and just fell over from a heart attack. You were a widower at fifty-two, I was a widow at forty-eight." And she told him her story.

He offered to walk her out to her car, and she agreed. The sun was just setting when they reached it, and they stood there talking for some time. Finally, he said, "I assume you probably have to go to get up early for work in the morning. " He hesitated for a second, then asked in a quiet voice, "Would you like to have dinner on Saturday night?" and she answered, "Yes, that would be nice." They exchanged phone numbers and departed.

During the week, while he visited various sights around Philadelphia, he thought about Elaine Chang. He found it interesting that she was very much like him, in education, temperament, experiences. The fact that they had both lost their spouses, and were still adjusting to single life again. One day, as he wandered around the Philadelphia Zoo, a thought occurred to him: he wondered if it was more than just a coincidence that they met. He decided to let things unfurl as they came, not to get his hopes up or his imagination too far abroad.

The dinner on Saturday night went well; he told her of his travels and the revelations concerning his family, and afterwards, she asked if he would like to attend another concert. He replied yes, and she told him where and when to meet. It was at a community center in Phoenixville, not far from King of Prussia. He enjoyed it as much as he did the first one, and they went out to dinner again afterwards. He had originally planned to stay in the Philadelphia area for only about two weeks, but now extended his itinerary. While she taught at the elementary school, he roamed the streets of Philadelphia, taking in the art and history museums, learning more about the Revolutionary War than he had ever known. As the sun rose earlier in the sky every morning and disappeared later every evening, he came to soak up its warmth and light. It made him feel much more energetic and buoyant. He imagined at times that he was a great eagle, flying above the clouds, looking down on the Earth and all its people. Deep inside, he felt and also wondered if he was falling in love.

One Saturday they drove west to Lancaster, the center of Amish country; she told him that she went there about once a month to browse through the great market and fill up the car with homemade foods and crafts. They enjoyed the day wandering through the city, occasionally stopping to look at a quilt or buy a loaf of homemade bread. On the ride back to Philadelphia, she told him of her week.

"My daughter called me the other night, and said, 'Mom, is something happening to you? Are you actually seeing someone?' I just said, 'maybe,' and left it at that."

He smiled and replied, "Is this what I have to look forward to when I get back to California? You just have one daughter. I have two, and they'll both probably be trying to set me up with someone. In my case, at least, there's no rest for the wicked."

She laughed. "Daughters are like that. They think that their parent should never be without a companion. Mothering instincts, I guess. Christine's been trying to get me with someone ever since Nelson died. She thinks, and I realize she means well, that I shouldn't be alone. I just tell her I can take care of myself. Eliot is more laid back. 'Mom will find the right person in the right time, that's up to her, not us,' he tells Christine. 'Just leave her alone, she'll be okay.'"

"Do you ever feel like remarrying? I've been in this position for a little over a year. You've had a lot more practice."

"I don't really know. I think that, at first, you try to compare everyone to your late spouse, and that's really kind of unfair. I knew Nelson since he was my brother's classmate in college. I loved him and everything that he was, but that's doesn't necessarily mean that I want to meet and go out with someone just like him." She was silent and thoughtful for a moment while she drove. "In a way, even though it's been over four years, I'm still attached to him, and maybe always will be at some level. I don't know. Does that make sense?"

"I think so. After all, I would think that when a person has been a major part of your life for so long, he or she becomes kind of ingrained, always there. I guess it's how to live with remembering one person and living your life with another. I don't know if I'm at that point yet."

"Really, I don't think I am either. But I know that I want to be beyond mourning, beyond the widow-in-black stage. Actually, Chinese widows are supposed to wear white, not black, but it amounts to the same thing."

"That's kind of what I'm looking for as well."

"Maybe then we're both on the same road, going in the same direction."

119

She talked about her early life as they drove. "I was born and raised in Brooklyn; my parents still live there; they're very old school Chinese. My father came here from Shanghai with my grandparents in 1946, after the war; they could see that the Communists were going to take over eventually. My mother's family was originally from Hong Kong. My brother Samuel was the genius of the family. He got into the Bronx High School of Science; have you heard of it?" He shook his head no, and she went on. "Very prestigious, very high powered. A kid who was in the class just ahead of Samuel's won the Nobel chemistry prize a few years ago. Anyway, Samuel went on to MIT, and met Nelson, who became one of his best friends; that's how Nelson and I originally connected. Samuel's now vice-president of an engineering firm in New York, has three children and four grandchildren. I was the dutiful daughter. I stayed at home and took the subway to New York City College for five years. I majored in music education, and married Nelson three weeks after I graduated. He studied economics at MIT, then went to business school at Columbia, and afterwards was recruited by an investment bank in Philadelphia. That's how we ended up here. I got pregnant about a year after getting married; Christine came first, then Eliot three years later. When they were both old enough to go to school, I enrolled in the graduate music program at Temple and got a master's degree. While Nelson worked, I gave private lessons. After he died, a friend of mine recommended me for a teaching job, so I still have a few private students, and teach strings to second, third, and fourth graders."

He told her about his own teaching experiences, and the fact that he and Beatrice had some of the same students. "I would get them for World History in tenth grade, and again in U.S. History as juniors, and sometimes in AP History as seniors. When they graduated, I'm sure, in fact I know, they said, 'No more Mr. Lindstrom and his essays and tests.' I know that because I read it in some of their yearbooks when I was asked to sign them. Then they went to the junior college and found out that Beatrice was their freshman honors writing teacher. She said they were aghast the first day they walked into her classroom and learned who she was." He grinned, and they both laughed as she drove on.

That night, at a restaurant in Philadelphia, they talked more about their lives, and reminisced about their travel experiences. Besides Chinese, Elaine spoke fluent French, and had been to Paris four times and Rome and London twice each, among other places. He talked about his years of chaperoning student groups to Europe, and taught her a few phrases of German, the language he knew best after English. He also told her the story of a disastrous experience in a Hong Kong restaurant when he and Beatrice toured China several years earlier: "We had been

120

traveling in China for two weeks, and all of our meals were pretty much Chinese food, which was overall pretty good. But the hotel that we stayed in in Hong Kong at the end of the tour had an American restaurant, so a bunch of us in the group went to it for dinner. I ordered a big cheeseburger, and waited almost an hour to get it. When it finally came, I grabbed a pot of mustard and spread it all over the burger. But when I bit into it, I realized that it was not regular American type mustard, but hot Chinese mustard. Every bite was sheer agony, but I finished it all. Beatrice was watching the expressions on my face and laughing at every bite."

He tried to repeat the few Chinese phrases that he still remembered, and she smiled at his attempts and corrected him. They both ended up laughing over his efforts, and when they left and walked into the Philadelphia night, she took his hand and held on to it all the way to the car.

The following week, she told him that she had a concert on Saturday night, but suggested that they do something on Sunday. He surprised her. "If you don't mind, let's go to the coast. I've seen enough of the Pacific; I want to go out to the Atlantic coast. I've been there only once briefly on this trip"

"Here, we call it the Shore. So you want to go to the Jersey Shore?"

"Yes. Is that okay with you?"

"Sounds wonderful. Actually, I haven't been there in a while myself."

Sunday morning he picked her up and they drove out of Philadelphia, across the Delaware River and through the numerous small communities that made up southwest New Jersey. After a time, the urban areas gave way to piney woods which almost, but not quite, reminded him of the great conifer forests of northern California. Only the flatness of the land helped him realize that they were far away from the West. In time, the salt air breeze told him that they were approaching the ocean, and after a while, and another barrier of developments, they saw the ocean. He drove along the beach, found a parking spot, got out, stared at the water for a minute, and then commented facetiously, "No, not like the Pacific. Too calm, too mellow. I like crashing waves and thundering surf. You call this an ocean?" He looked at her in mock amazement. She laughed, a warm hearty caring laugh, and the sky and the gulls soaring in it suddenly seemed insignificant.

They spent the day meandering through little coastal towns, venturing in and out of curio and craft shops, playing tourist, and occasionally doing silly touristy things like walking barefoot in the beach sand, going down to the water, then dashing back up when the tide came in. they picked up seashells and rocks, and found pieces of sea glass which they put in their pockets. They drove a bit north to Barnegat Light, and climbed the stairs to the top of the lighthouse, and looked out at the vast Atlantic. She again took his hand and held it in hers, and they stared together, their views reaching to the horizon.

They found a little restaurant in a town by the name of Seaside Park, located right on the shore, and had the best seafood dinner he had ever tasted. He told her what he planned to do after leaving Philadelphia, and she mentioned upcoming music concerts and a visit to her parents in Brooklyn. They talked openly and freely and let all their hopes and visions come forth while they ate and drank. Afterwards they went down to the beach and walked along it, and watched the dusk come over it like warm and comforting shadows. He suddenly felt as if he had to ask her something, even though he thought he knew what the answer would be.

"Elaine, I'm almost afraid to ask, and I know that you have to work tomorrow, but if you could, would you like to spend the night here with me?"

She looked at him, and then took his face in her hands and kissed him. "Actually, that sounds nice. Yes, I would like that. Let's do it."

"But you have to be at school."

She replied with decisiveness. "I haven't taken a day off from school in over three years. I have so much sick and personal leave time stored up that I might as well start using it. I think I can play hooky for a day." She paused and looked at him. "That was hard for you to ask, wasn't it?"

He nodded, and she took his arm, and they walked along the beach some more, and she lay her head on his shoulder, and quietly said, "If you had not asked that first, I might have. Michael, I want to start living again. I haven't been like that in a long while, but ever since I met you, I feel like I've been waking up, and now it's time."

Eventually, as it was getting dark, they turned around, and she steered him back to the parking lot where the Toyota was located. In the car, she turned to him, and said, "Don't feel bad about asking me. It was hard for me to answer, too."

As they drove, he said one more thing. "I want to be honest with you. I can't promise you that I'll stay here. With the other things I need to do and the commitments I've made I have to leave in the next week or so, and what will happen after that, I just don't know. That's all I can say. Do you still want to go through with what I proposed?"

She said," Yes," And they said nothing more as they drove into the darkness.

They found a small but clean hotel on the shore road across from the beach. While he took a shower, she used her smartphone to arrange for a sub and send in lesson plans for her classes the next day. Then she turned off the phone and put it aside and forgot about it. Finally, she readied herself, and they settled into a bed of soft comfortable sheets and warm blankets and took each other. And at the end, they fell asleep, her head resting against his chest, and let the rest of the world attend to its own larger affairs.

In the early morning, well before dawn, with darkness still outside, he suddenly woke up and jumped out of bed. She awoke and sat up, startled.

"Michael, what's the matter?"

"I just thought of it a minute ago. I've never seen the sun rise over the ocean in the morning. I've seen it set over the Pacific in the evening plenty of times, but never rise over the Atlantic."

She looked at the clock on the nightstand. "But it's only four a.m.. It won't be up for at least another hour, probably longer."

He stopped. She turned on the light, and as she did, the sheet dropped from her hands, revealing her warm golden body, finely textured skin and arms, and soft curved breasts. She held out her hand, and said softly, "Come back to bed." He did, and they started all over again.

An hour and a half later, they did get dressed and walked down to the beach, the sky was still greyish blue, the air was misty chilled, but on the ocean horizon they could see the first glimmer of dawn. Far in the distance, the sun peaked over the water, opened its lids and then within a few minutes burst forth in dazzling splendor that hit them and flooded warmth through their bodies. They held each other as the power and the fury surged through them. She closed her eyes, and thought she fell asleep for a minute. Then he was shaking her, and asking if she'd like to go somewhere for breakfast.

After they ate, they returned to the hotel room and packed up what few things they had. As they left, he turned to her and said, "I feel like I have to apologize. I feel like I've corrupted you. I hope I haven't."

She laughed and then grew somber. "I did have an affair with a man about a year after Nelson's death. I thought I was ready, but I wasn't. Even though I tried not to be, I felt cold and dead. I broke it off after about six weeks and really haven't been serious with anyone since. Until now. You've made me feel warm again."

He took her hand. "And you've helped me as well."

"Tonight Christine will probably call and say, 'Mom, I tried to get in touch with you yesterday and last night. Where were you?' And I may just tell her, 'I spent the night in bed with a man I've known for all of three weeks.' It'll probably freak her out."

They drove back to Philadelphia, to her home near Phoenixville, west of the City. "Home" was in a small but comfortable complex, a three bedroom condominium. She told him, "When Nelson and I were married and the kids were growing up, we had a five bedroom house on an acre of property about ten miles from here. But after he died, I just didn't feel like living there anymore. I didn't need it anyway; the kids were pretty much elsewhere and the place felt hollow. I sold it two years ago and bought this; it's just about the right size and a lot closer to where I teach."

He escorted her up the sidewalk to her front door, and waited until she had her key out. Then she turned and kissed him and held him close to her for several minutes. "Thank you, Michael, thank you for everything. You don't know how much this has meant to me." She looked at him and asked, "How much longer will you be in the area?"

He turned fidgety, stumbled for a minute, and then hoarsely replied, "I should probably get going by Friday at the latest."

"Can you come over Thursday evening for dinner, then?"

"Certainly."

I'll call you before then, but Thursday for sure." She kissed him again, opened the door, and went in. He walked back to the Toyota.

On Thursday at six, he showed up at her house with a bottle of wine. She greeted him at the door, and led him inside. The living room was softly furnished with a sofa and recliner chair in earth tones, oak end tables, and lithographic prints. An upright piano was against one of the walls, with a modernistic, almost abstract, picture of Bach over it. On a bookshelf were framed pictures of her daughter and son. Inviting smells came from the kitchen-dining room.

"Here, sit down and be comfortable, "she said as she took the wine from his hands. "Dinner will be in a few minutes. Would you like something to drink?"

"No thank you."

While she finished up the meal, they talked about their day. He had taken another trip to Valley Forge, to walk among the trees and absorb the land and the men who had encamped there. She had taught at the elementary school from 8:30 until 2:30, third graders. He laughed when she mimicked the grating and ear-piercing sounds that came from beginner violins and violas. "It's probably what I would sound like if I tried to play right now."

"Well, they'll get better. It takes time and practice. I can't expect them to be masters in a few months. I remember when I first picked up the violin at age six. I know I sounded awful. It took quite a while for me to get to the point where I could play something recognizable. Here, I'm finished. Come sit down and eat."

She had set her small round dinner nook table formally, with her best plates and silverware. He was surprised at the lengths she went to and told her, "You didn't need to go through all this trouble. I've never been this formal, not even when Beatrice and I were entertaining. "

She put her fingers over his lips. "Hush, no more. I want to do this."

The food was equally impressive. She had made a chicken and rice dish, steamed vegetables, and ciabatta rolls. It was delicious, the best food he had eaten in some time, followed by carrot cake. Between that, and the wine, by the end of the meal, he was bright and relaxed, feeling warm and soft, and he had the idea that she was, too.

He helped her clear the dishes, but she told him to stay in the living room while she cleaned up. He sat in the semi-light reading a music magazine, when she came out of the kitchen. "Ta-da. Finished. Now, wait here. I want to give you something special for a sendoff."

She left the room for a minute, and then came back with her violin case and a folder of sheet music. She set up the music stand, tuned her instrument, ran through some chords, and then began to play the most beautiful version of Pachelbel he had ever heard. It went on and on, and as the notes reached his mind and then his heart, he felt as if they were lifting him up and taking him away to a great place in the eternal blue sky. He was mesmerized by her performance, and felt helpless to tell her to stop. The Pachelbel floated into Bach, and then into Handel and his world became her and her ethereal sounds spinning through the air. When she finally stopped, well beyond an hour, he was still suspended.

She put down the violin and sat next to him and put her arms around him and pulled him close. After several minutes, she whispered, "Come." He realized what she had in mind, and protested. "But you have to get up early tomorrow. Are you sure you'll get enough sleep?"

"Michael, I don't know when the next time I'll see you will be. I want to remember you, I want to remember you for a long time." She turned off the living room light and led him by the hand to her bedroom. There, she pulled back the covers, silently bade him to undress, then undressed herself. Before getting onto bed, she left a small nightlight glowing, and in its shadow, they made love until well after midnight, and then drifted away into dreamful sleep.

In the early morning, he was in her bathroom washing himself, when he heard her rise. When he come out, she was there in a bathrobe, and escorted him to the door. She turned to him and said, "I'd like you to stay for breakfast, but I really do need to get ready for school."

"That's all right. There's a pancake and waffle place just down from my motel. After I pack up and check out, I'll get something there."

"How far do you think you'll get today?"

"I'd like to spend the next few days at Gettysburg, and then go to Antietam and from there to D.C."

"Michael, please be safe. I want us to see each other again."

"I do, too. I'll be careful. I'll call you when I get there."

She looked at him intently. "I'm jealous that Beatrice had you for so long. She was probably the luckiest woman on earth."

He blushed. "Thank you. Thank you for everything, Elaine."

They took each other's hands and stood looked into their faces for a second. Then they kissed again, and let go of their hands, and he opened the door, looked at her once more, and walked out. He heard the door quietly closing behind him. The sun was peering over the horizon as he climbed into the Toyota.

Interlude Four

He spent the day driving through the southern Pennsylvania countryside, and that night, since the weather by now was warm and sunny, found a small campground outside Gettysburg. After dinner, he wrote and sent an email to Laura and Danae, telling them about meeting Elaine and his relationship with her, although he left certain parts out of it. He wanted to write them down, commit them to paper, to assure himself that they had actually happened, but he also wanted to know what his daughters' reactions would be, in the event that they might eventually have a stepmother.

Both replied within an hour. Danae's reaction was to the effect of, "Dad, go for it!" but then Danae was the much more romantic of the two. Danae was a seeker of adventure and possibility. She had changed her major three times in college, had already gone through two boyfriends since high school, and would no doubt experience several more before settling down, if she ever did. Even then, he wondered if Danae might be married and divorced several times in her life, her husbands not quite understanding the allure of the unknown and esoteric in her. He had the idea that Danae would mature into someone like Denise: in love with life beyond the horizon, traveling the world looking for the perfect episode, all the while contributing to and helping others. A good and rewarding path, he concluded, but not the one that he would have chosen.

Laura was more restrained and measured, not unexpected, since she was older and infinitely more grounded and mature than Danae. Laura, he thought, was much like her grandfather, Stephen Lindstrom from Swensen and St. Louis. She had always been grown up, even as a child. She always volunteered to help around the house, she was the head of the youth group at church, and eventually senior class president in high school. She worked with several school service groups, seeing the world not as people thought it should be, but as it was, and trying to improve it from there. Even in college, along with her classes and studies, she became involved in a club that helped the homeless, and another that went into schools to work with children who had reading problems. She and Steve had dated for almost three years before she agreed that he was the right young man: hard working, morally upright, caring and dedicated; for her. In fact, she decided to marry him, and not the other way around. In many ways, her reply was what he expected it to be: "Mom has been gone for a little over a year, and you probably still feel some grief. I want you to be happy, and it sounds like Elaine has given you happiness, or at least an absence of pain. I'm glad that you met her, and, yes, you should stay in touch with her. But I would also say that you should probably wait a while before advancing this to the next level, make sure that it's genuine and real, and it's what both of you want. I think that if you do that, you'll find true happiness. Also, don't worry about feeling unfaithful to Mom. She would want you to meet someone good for you, she would want you to continue with your life, and enjoy it as much as possible. You're not being unfaithful at all. You're simply being human. Love you, Dad."

He sat back in his camp chair and ruminated on Laura's words. Someone so young, yet so wise and understanding. In any event, he had time. He would probably not see Elaine for some time, although he presumed and hoped they would keep in touch. And there were so many other things for him to do over the next few months. It amused him that he was now turning to his children for personal advice, and, in effect, asking them for permission to continue with the woman that he had met. Things have come full circle, he thought. He remembered when they were teens, listening to their anxieties and passions concerning boys that they barely knew. The girls would tell him only so much, of course, and Beatrice, with her feminine intuition, would fill in the rest when they met in bed in the evening. At the time, he saw their concerns as minor blips on the screens of their lives, but to them, he knew, they were major upheavals. Each one seemed more dramatic than the last, and not until they started seriously dating at fifteen or sixteen did he understand the complexity and the cost of relationships to girls. Even when Laura and Steve announced their engagement years later, when both were in their mid-twenties, he could see that trauma beneath the happiness, and came to realize how precious it was: something not to be taken lightly.

He kept Laura's reply in a cubbyhole in his mind for possible future use, added another entry to his journal, watched the spring constellations in their seasonal treks across the sky, finally called it a night, and fell asleep in the back of the Toyota.

In the morning, he wrote back to each of them, thanking them for their responses and his own reaction to them, and then drove to the Gettysburg National Military Park visitor's center for an introduction to the site that changed the course of American, and perhaps world, history.

May

He entered the Washington D.C. area the same as he had left Philadelphia, under a sky so blue that he wondered if it was on a canvas instead of merely being above him. It guided and reflected his path into the capital area as he approached it from the north.

A week before, he halted and spent time in Gettysburg, Pennsylvania. He had never been to Gettysburg before, and the history and significance of the town piqued his interest. After all, he had taught the Battle of Gettysburg many times in the American History class, prodding students to imagine the fighting at Cemetery Ridge and the futility of Pickett's Charge. Here, he explained, were two great generals, Lee and Meade, in a battle which would essentially decide the fate of the war. Here were the largest armies which would ever see combat up to the time. Here the Union stopped Lee's Confederate advance into the North, and threw him back into Virginia, giving Lincoln the chance to make good on his promise to hold the country together. Here, too, the President, following Senator Everett's two hour address, spoke for only three minutes, about two hundred words. Never was so much said with such limited diction and syntax. So much turned here. He wandered around the various points of the battlefield for three days, the same time, he noted that the two armies fought each other, saw the memorials and the markers, walked where soldiers had trod, and visited where skirmishes decided the hour. When he left, he felt as if he could have been a member of the Minnesota Volunteers or the Army of Northern Virginia, marching to face off the enemy. He left Gettysburg much more somber than when he arrived.

Now he was traveling to Washington, D.C., the city that the Union had to hold in order to win the war. That it did hold was a matter of both firearms and faith. But the fact was that it held. He found a campground on the outskirts of the town, near Alexandria, moved himself in for an extended stay, and began the process of rediscovering the nation's capital.

He had been to Washington, D.C. previously, but never as a simple tourist. Once he had come for a history conference, in which he and others had been bused around to a few of the more interesting and touristy sights: the Lincoln Memorial, the Jefferson Memorial, the Capitol building (for a quick and salutatory tour), and the Vietnam Veteran's Memorial. Lincoln's great visage overlooking the reflecting pool and the Mall impressed him the most, a man larger than life, coming from a homespun wilderness background to lead the nation in the most devastating conflict it had ever known, succeeding, and then

129

dying on the morning of his triumph. Lincoln did belong to the ages, as perhaps the most representative of all Americans, either before or after. Something in the man made him take off his hat and put it over this chest as he saw the Memorial once again. It was not facetious or condescending, but the inner spirit that recognized a higher compass of the national mind, he thought, and he would afterwards use Lincoln as the model if anyone else tried to declare a person as "great."

Now, crossing the Potomac River, he toured the city once more, and with more ease, as he had the time for a more thorough exploration. He visited the National Air and Space Museum, saw the Apollo 11 capsule, the Bell X-1, SpaceShip 1, and other craft which had defied the Earth. He wandered introspectively through the National Art Gallery, with its Da Vincis and Gaugins and Pissarros; and he also made a pilgrimage to the National Archives, where, in a darkened room full of security, he viewed the original documents of freedom: the handwritten and fading Declaration of Independence, on which he noted the signers: Jefferson, Franklin, Adams, Lee (two of them, he remembered, the great uncles of Robert E. of Gettysburg), McKean, Rodney, Hall, and many others, and the almost as old but still very readable Constitution. Next to these were two other framed documents, each a testament to the values of Western Civilization. One, a few years younger, the Bill of Rights, the product of George Mason, who felt that the Constitution did not go far enough; the other, retreating to an era of knights and swords, far before the Revolution, a 1297 copy of the Magna Carta, the document which first enunciated the rights of people. These four great treatises together, he thought, so little in writing, so much in power and dignity.

Another day he visited the Capitol, on the Hill, with its Classical Style dome rising above the skyline. After patiently enduring the security checks, he joined a tour group that wandered through the great building, from the House side to the Senate. While the guide droned on in his ear, he meandered aimlessly, eyes glancing across the walls and through the hallways. He thought he saw Daniel Webster talking to a colleague while briskly walking through a corridor, and Henry Clay disappearing through a doorway. In another secluded area, he imagined John Calhoun, fiery and unrepentant, arguing with an opponent; and Jefferson Davis, senator from Mississippi before he became President of the Confederacy, somber and solemn. Agree with them or not, they were people of stature, he thought, and today's alleged titans paled in comparison to them. Then, he realized, senators like McCain and Leahy and Hatch will be considered giants to the people a hundred years from now.

The next day was a visit to the war memorials. To him, they were surreal, rising from the Earth itself and presenting themselves to humans as if molded by the gods to remind them of their folly. The Vietnam Veteran's Memorial was a great slash in the ground, disrupting the elements. He walked along its black marble façade and glanced at the names on it, each one of a life lost in time and space. After a long search, he came across the inscription of a second cousin, a man he had never met, but had heard about over the years, who died at Pleiku in 1967. He ran his hands over the inscription that read "Thomas Lindstrom," and felt his core grow soft and vulnerable. One of his own was on this wall, and he felt connected to the rest of the names as well.

The Korean War Veteran's Memorial, he was much less attracted to, perhaps because it was personally more removed from him. He knew the conflict mostly as pages in the history books that he taught, and its significance, although important, did not affect him as much. It was a dream drifting away on the sleep of night, and when he awoke, he would remember it, but only as fleeting visions in his mind. Even its solidity here at the patches of ground along the Potomac did not bring emotion to him; unlike Gettysburg, these were merely symbols, not the instruments themselves.

The World War II memorial was much more real to him. His father had fought in the War, had participated in D-Day, marched through Paris the afternoon it was liberated, and was on the banks of the Elbe River when Germany surrendered. He had been only one of millions who had saved Europe from Nazi tyranny, but he did his part, and then came home. His father never talked much about the war, the death and destruction he had seen, but people remembered. He once told Michael that after retiring, he and his wife visited the Normandy beaches during a trip to France. When the local French learned that he was a D-Day veteran, they went out of their way to guide him around the area, refused pay for his meals, and gave him a going-away dinner. After all those years, people remembered.

He drove to Richmond one day. Richmond, like its historical counterpart, had much to offer, and after he settled into a motel, he decided to explore. Jefferson Davis' home during the war, the Confederate White House, the building where the Confederate legislature met, the Confederate hospital, and the various foundries that supplied war materials. One day he drove down to Petersburg to see the fortifications used in the siege of the city, and the church on the outskirts of the town, now a memorial to the states that fought for the South, with its Tiffany stained-glass windows. As he visited the area, he pondered that this was the last gasp of the South: that once Petersburg was broken, Richmond fell, and Lee's army began its journey west to eventual surrender at the McLean House in Appomattox.

Finally, at the end of the week, returning to the D.C. area, and after a boat trip to Mt. Vernon, he willed himself to cross the river and journey to Arlington. The land that the cemetery now occupied, he knew, had belonged to the Custis family before the Civil War. George Washington Parke Custis was the adopted grandson of George Washington, and he inherited the estate when his grandfather died. He and his wife had one surviving child, Mary, who eventually married a young Army officer, Robert E. Lee. The estate was seized by Union forces at the beginning of the war and put to use as a cemetery for Union dead. It had grown from there. He knew this already, but read it at the front entrance, and mentioned to the guard that it was ironic that Lee never owned slaves and really didn't believe in slavery, but fought for the South anyway. "You must be a historian," the man replied, "But, then most people who come here think they are." The guard grinned, and he went on his way.

After picking up a guide at the visitor's center, he walked through the rows of upright standing monuments among the trees. A minute later, a grey marble monument caught his attention, one with five stars on it. Five star generals were rare, he thought; there were only about four of five of them, all from World War II. He made his way to the stone and read the name on it: "Omar Bradley." The "GI General" he thought, and the last of the five star officers to die. A little piece of history here. But then, he thought, everything in this place was a bit of history in one way or another. As he moved on into the depths of the necropolis, he noted and paused at other markers: Matthew Henson, the companion of Robert E. Peary on his North Pole expeditions; General George C. Marshall, Roosevelt's Chief of Staff during World War II; Claire Chennault, who commanded the "Flying Tigers" squadron in China during WWII; Michael DeBakey, the famous heart surgeon; Earl Warren, whose name was forever attached to Brown vs. Board of Education; Charles Conrad, the third man to walk on the Moon; Gary Powers, who created an international crisis by being shot down over the Soviet Union in a U-2 spy plane.

He passed these and many more before he came to a rise just below the Arlington House property. Here he stopped and read the memorial plaques set into stone next to a gas generated flame. This, he already know, as the resting place of John F. Kennedy, his two brothers, his wife, and two of his children. He remembered that day in November 1963, when he and his family had watched on television the president's death and funeral. Now, almost fifty years later, he was at the site. Kennedy had not been as great a man as Lincoln, but he had tinges of

132

greatness, and he may well have gone on to do major things if he had not been assassinated. On the other hand, the stories concerning his personal life that came out after his death may have limited any notion of his fame for posterity. He shook his head and wondered on What If.

From the Kennedy gravesite, he looked out on the vista of Washington D.C. in the distance. Before him, the entire city spread out, with the U.S. Capitol, the Washington monument, the Lincoln Memorial, the Mall outlined in sharp relief against a vast cloudless blue sky. The whole of the United States government and heritage was before him. He had read that Kennedy, before he was killed, had come to this place at one time, and reportedly said, "I could stay here forever." It reminded him of once when he and Beatrice, early in their marriage, had gone to Yosemite and he talked her into hiking to the top of Half Dome, that imposing shard of granite overlooking the Valley. They began in the early morning, and trudged uphill, past Vernal Falls, then past Nevada Falls and little Yosemite Valley, into the early afternoon, over eight miles of dusty angled trail, their feet sore and leg muscles burning from the exertion and the altitude. Then came the cables on the side of the Dome, pulling up, one arm length at a time until their arms and hands ached and there were no more steps and they were on top. It was exhausting, but the view was worth it. They could look out over the entire Valley, see the Sierra Nevadas, snowcapped even in June, rising to the east, and the brown of the Central Valley to the west, almost all the way to the Pacific Ocean. There was no sound but for the wind and the hushed talk of other hikers, and above it all the overwhelming mountain sky. Beatrice, as she took in the sight, exclaimed, "If I could, I would build a cabin here and stay for the rest of my life."

Now, as he stood on the grassy area next to the graves, he could hear the distant rumble of vehicles on the Beltway surrounding D.C., but at the cemetery itself, there was only the sound of the wind tuning the just starting to leaf tree branches, and he liked it. This was not a place for laughter or loud talk or noise, he thought. He remembered that some ten years before, he had led a student trip to France. They visited the American cemetery in Normandy on the hill above Omaha Beach, then a group of students took the steps down to the beach itself. He followed them, and when he got there, he noticed that they were playing in the surf, laughing and running around. He called them together and told them, "There are very few truly sacred places on Earth and this is one of them. Over two thousand American soldiers died on this beach on D-Day morning. These sands are full of American blood." They were much quieter and more somber after that. Arlington is the same way, he thought to himself. This is a sacred place.

133

A short walk up the hill and he was at the mansion itself. Gravestones were all around it: in the front yard, the back, the garden, the bushes, everywhere. It was said, he heard, that the Union wanted to make sure that this property, no matter what happened after the war, would never be returned to the Custis-Lee family. After the war, the Lee family sued to have it returned, and the Supreme Court eventually upheld their claim. Since the area was already a cemetery, they sold it back to the U.S. government and never lived there again.

He walked around the mansion and took the road that led to the main amphitheater due south. Just before it, he stopped at the Challenger and Columbia memorials, honoring the crews of the ill-fated space shuttles. He looped around the amphitheater, and came out on its east side to a wide open plaza that sloped down. Here he came upon a crowd, quiet and reverent. He checked his watch and knew what was happening. It was the changing of the guard at the Tomb of the Unknown Soldier. He saw the inspection of arms, the removal of one guard and entrance of another, and the walk down the pathway, twenty-one steps one way, twenty-one the other, in front of a white marble sepulcher that gleamed in the early spring sun. Then it was over.

He had one more place to visit that morning. After the ceremony at the Tomb of the Unknown Soldier, he found and walked down Porter Drive. The air was crisp and the wind was like cool fingers wrapping themselves around him. He thought that he saw colors, the blue of the sky, the green of the lawns, the browns of the trees, and above all, the whites of the gravestones sharper and more focused than they would have been somewhere else. Maybe it was just his imagination, maybe it was something else. Maybe many something elses.

Eventually, as he transitioned from Porter Drive to Bradley Drive, his eye caught a marker among the greens which read "Section 60." He started looking for row numbers as he continued through the street. Shortly before Marshall Drive, he came to the row he was looking for and turned left and walked silently among the stones. He read the names and dates of birth and death as he passed by them. This section, as he already knew, was reserved for soldiers who had been killed in Afghanistan and Iraq, or killed in the war on terrorism. The death dates were recent: 2002, 2004, 2008, 2010, 2009. Their spirits had not been gone for long.

Finally, he came to one stone and stopped. He crouched down and read it carefully, taking in all of the message on it, although it said, like all the others, little enough: CPL Jason M. Lindstrom, b. September 7, 1982, d. May 5, 2003, Afghanistan. That was all. He gazed at it for several minutes, almost oblivious to other people who were making their own searches and finds near him. He could only feel their movements, not see or hear them. He stared at the date of death again. It was almost nine years to the day when his nephew, in a war-torn faraway place, breathed his last, and then came home. And he had never met him. He closed his eyes for a minute, and the world disappeared, and then he opened them again, and the world was still there. For him.

Jane had told him that Jason had been so much like his father, a free thinker, a seeker of rightness and justice, a believer in standing up for the oppressed. She said that he had gone to Afghanistan to try to right a wrong. At first, his parents did not want him to go, that the military was wasteful and destructive. But then they realized that he was seeking the same goal that they had over twenty years earlier, and they would be hypocrites if they refused him. And he went. And eventually came home to rest. Jason's resting spot was perhaps one of the most peaceful places on Earth, he thought as he walked down the hill and to the Toyota in the visitor's parking lot. A short distance away, he heard the sound of taps on a bugle as another soldier was laid down, another warrior who had come home to sleep in this place of green and blue and white.

Beatrice would have liked this place, he thought. Not the signs of death, but the solitude and the calm and the warmth and the healing. People no longer suffered here, they lay in peace and quiet. Their spirits were soothed. The violence and damage done to their bodies no longer mattered. Under the blossoming trees and the flowers and shrubs and the sky and the silence, she would see this as a place of endearment. This was not just a cemetery, but a great landscape where memories were kept and recollected, where people could come and be reminded of those that they loved and cherished and why they were loved and cherished. Beatrice would not have found death here at Arlington, but life and beauty.

As he walked away, he saw a grey-haired woman and a bald-headed man, perhaps in their 60s, wandering among the rows of stones, searching, peering intently, and then finally stopping at one. He noticed them kneeling down and touching the marker as he had done. He thought of how many times this same scene played out every day, not only at Arlington, but at military cemeteries though out the country, and all over the world as well. He thought of going up and sharing their grief, and then decided to let them be. They were only a few minutes, and after they left, he wandered over and read the stone that they were at. Specialist Winston Gaines April 10, 1982-April 26, 2004 Iraq. Not much older than Jason in a faraway place that until then few Americans had heard of, much less imagined. He thought of reading some others, then looked up and down the rows and saw hundreds of stones. He turned and walked out of the lawn and down the hill to the parking lot.

As he drove away, he glanced at his rear view mirror, and saw the white markers among the grass and trees, and decided that this was where America really was. These were the abodes of the dead so that the nation might continue. There were bitter debates, he knew, about the morality and politics and economics of war. Arlington and other military cemeteries, though, were ground zero as far as those arguments were concerned, and would be for generations to come. As long as human beings had differences, as long as they tried to solve those differences with action, places like Arlington would be necessary to remind them of what the cost was.

At the campground, he was tired. He walked to a small diner not far away, had a meal of a sandwich, salad, and bread, and then walked back, oblivious to the traffic and the commuter trains and the bicyclists. He composed an email to Elaine, wrote in his journal until he could barely keep his eyes open, then put it aside, sent his usual "I'm doing well" message to his daughters, and called it a night.

June

And so the traveler returned to his adopted land.

He followed the sun, driving west, keeping his heart and mind on the vast open skies. From Washington D.C., he crossed through Maryland, southwest Pennsylvania, and then followed Interstate 70 across Ohio and Indiana, following the ancient paths. Then he turned north, to Chicago, and from there, up into Wisconsin and back into Minnesota, to the timeless Great Plains Country. After he left Boston in March, after the revelations of his sister and brother's lives, he backtracked and returned to Buffalo. Now, he was fulfilling a promise that he made to both Susan and Jane Andrews. He reached the town of Swensen in the evening, as he had done almost six months before. But it and its surroundings were very different. The fields, everywhere he could see, were full of corn and wheat, vast acreages spanning from one end of the horizon to the other. The land was alive with growth and maturity. He took a room at the same hotel he had stayed at in January. Without the snow and the greyness, it looked fresh and new, ready to meet all challenges. He did not plan to stay long, and, so, the next morning, he drove out of town to the old farmhouse and barn that were his grandparents' legacy. This June day they were half hidden by the growth in the fields. He took a box and a shovel out of the back of the Toyota, and walked down the broken gravel driveway to the two weathered buildings. When he got to them, all was silent, only the quiet talk of the wind through the broken boards and the scream of a hawk in the airy distance and the swaying of the corn. From the box, he pulled out a while porcelain urn and scattered its contents around the outside of the barn, the house, and in the immediate fields. After he finished, he stood back, silent, for a minute, and turning into the barn, he found a corner where he dug a hole, and placed the urn with a picture in it. As he did, he heard a rustle and, looking up into a dark corner of the broken rafters, saw a Barn Owl staring down at him. He filled in the hole and walked away. He returned to Swensen, drove to the Lutheran Church, and for the second time that year, walked through the gate to the cemetery. He found his father's grave without difficulty, and placed on it a second photo, a copy of the first. He stood back, looking at the image, and said to himself, David, you've finally come home. Then he left. When he would return to Swensen, he did not know.

He called Elaine that night and told her what he had done, and how he felt about it. Then he journeyed south, retracing his steps to St. Louis. Denise greeted him with joy and happiness. That first night, they stayed up far into the darkness as he told her about his experiences and discoveries. He revealed Elaine to her; she was pleased that he had met her, and told him, "Michael, maybe you've found your partner for the rest of your life. People aren't meant to be alone." When he pointed out," You are," she shook her head, and replied, "I might be solitary, but I've never been alone, and I don't think ever will be. I have friends and students and so many other people that I know. I'll teach, I'm sure, until the day I die. When you were here in December, you were lost and lonely; I could tell it. After Beatrice died, you really had no one to share with. Now you do."

He replied, "I'm no longer afraid of getting back into a serious relationship, but there are so many strikes against it, starting with the fact that we live almost 3,000 miles apart. The last thing I'd want to do is ask to her abandon what she's known and done all her life just to be with me, or, in that case, vice versa. It simply wouldn't be fair."

Denise was thoughtful for a minute, and then she answered. "Many people are happily together who live in different parts of the country, or even the world. I have friends, academic couples who, because of their jobs, live apart much of the year. I know a professor at the university whose wife teaches at Baylor. They see each other at breaks and holidays and during the summer. Another teacher I know is at UMSL and her husband is at Iowa State. Happens all the time. Distance isn't a barrier anymore. Think about it." And they moved on to other subjects.

At breakfast the day after he arrived, he told Denise what he had learned about his parents and his brother. She was astonished by the story, and shook her head in both surprise and sympathy. "This is the first I've ever heard of this. My mother never said a word during all the years we were growing up. I'll bet she didn't even talk about this to my father." She was silent for a minute, then concluded, "Michael, probably every family has its secrets; some are big, others are small, but they're there and always have been, and they'll mark us in ways that we'll never totally understand."

One day, while Denise was teaching a summer class at the university, he walked around Forest Park. In contrast to December, it was green and vibrant and he enjoyed it. He took off his shoes and socks and mingled with the grass. In St. Louis, June was lovely, when the land was green and the sky was blue above, and the temperature was not yet full of the Mississippi Valley humidity of July and August that made everything so miserable. The trees were fully sculptured and the flower gardens were arrays of paint strokes of every hue and shade. As he walked by the Jewel Box, it exploded in diamond light that reflected off the trees and the grass and the sky around it. This is a wonderful time of year, he thought.

Denise invited Carmine Rickart to dinner a few days after he arrived. The young woman was delighted to see him, and started talking to him almost as soon as she was in the door. She was still at her parents' house, sorting through their possessions little by little. She missed them, she said, but he could tell that she was still young, and she would flourish without trouble. She told him about more of the stories she had written; she was still trying to get them published. At one point during the evening, she said that she had decided not to return to Duke in the fall, but in January would start attending Lindenwood, a small liberal arts college across the Missouri River near St. Charles. "I never really caught on to Duke," she told him. "I just wasn't happy there. I think I went there just because Mom and Dad wanted me to attend a 'prestigious' school. Well, I don't really care that much about so-called prestigious schools anymore. Maybe they're prestigious for some people, but not for me. I want to go someplace that fits me, not someone else."

When it came time for him to leave, Denise gave him a hug, and said in unconditional tones, "You've spent your whole life helping others, making others happy. I have never forgotten all those times when you were willing to listen to me on the phone for hours at a time. Now, this is your time. Don't forget that." And she all but shoved him out the door. He was laughing as he drove away.

From Missouri, he took the southern route, down through Oklahoma, where the grandparents and great-grandparents of so many of his students had fled from in the wake of the Dust Bowl. Today, it was, for the most part, still brown, but the land was being more wisely used, and there was little chance of another exodus in the wake of natural catastrophe. From Oklahoma City, he dropped down to Interstate 20 out of Fort Worth, and then west through the great Texas plains, a long, desolate, and unimaginably beautiful vista that stretched for hundreds of miles. As he drove, he felt himself the only person in the world. He eventually merged into Interstate 10, and only a short distance away was El Paso.

In an email to her query some weeks earlier, he had promised Luz that he would stop in El Paso on his way home, and he made good on it. The night he arrived, he called her from the hotel he was at; she was working, but had the next day off and, not requested, but demanded that he meet her for lunch at a café not far away. When she arrived, she grabbed and hugged him until he felt that they were going to embarrass the entire dining room. While they sat and ate, she talked almost constantly about her victories: she had passed the GED and was now signed up for college classes, only two a semester due to her work schedule. But she had met with a counselor, and, setting up a graduation timeline, learned that she could graduate from the junior college in three years, transfer to UTEP, and get an elementary teachers' credential in three more. In the meantime, she had secured a job as a teacher's aide at a school not far from her apartment; her days in the restaurant were coming to an end.

"Michael, I'm so excited. I feel like I'm someone completely new."

He talked to her about his travels, an abridged version, and she listened intently, stopping him every now and then only to make a comment. He told her about Elaine, and she was pleased that they had met each other and parted with the promise of possibly a more serious relationship. When lunch was over and they were getting ready to leave, she asked him how long he was going to stay in the area.

"Probably only another day or two. I have a few other places that I want to visit; after that I need to head home."

"Then you are going to have a good Mexican meal before you leave. My place tomorrow night."

He was at her modest but clean apartment at the appointed hour. Luz introduced him to her younger daughter Esperanza, a shy quiet girl of fifteen. During the dinner Esperanza said nothing, but when Luz went to serve dessert, he asked her about her school and classes. As first she was hesitant, but with his encouragement, she was soon talking freely about choir and biology, her two favorite subjects. She excused herself to do homework, and he wished her well in her studies. He helped Luz clean the table and the kitchen, and afterwards they sat in the small but clean living room and talked about their lives. She mentioned a man she had met at the junior college, a police officer studying for a criminology degree, and gone out with him once or twice, nothing serious, she said, but she felt he was a good person. They talked until he felt it was time to leave, close to midnight. She escorted him to the door, and then bade him goodnight and wished him a safe journey. She did not ask him to stay the night, and he did not want to ask it of her. She had once succored him when he was in pain, but now they were friends and nothing more.

He left El Paso the next morning and drove into New Mexico. He slipped through Albuquerque on Interstate 25, not stopping. Michelle Westerling had sent him emails about what her boys had told her concerning their father. The news was not good. Dan was still, as far as they could tell, on drugs, still resisting admonitions to go into rehab once more, still with his young women. He asked whether it would be worth it on his way home stop and try to talk some sense into him. Her answer was despondent. "I don't think there's any way anyone can help Dan anymore. He has to do it himself now. I've tried to help him, other people I know have, even some of his legal colleagues have. I don't think you'd make an impact on him, either. Maybe one of his playmates will. I don't know. Michael, it's best just to go home and get on with your life. I'll keep in touch." He stopped for the night in Colorado Springs, and continued north until he reached Cheyenne, Wyoming.

From there, he traveled to Laramie, where another college friend, now a petroleum engineer, lived. After the experience with Dan, it was good to see other people that he knew and loved being healthy and successful. He spent several days with Robert and his family, talking about old times, laughing at the goofy and inane things they did in college, and the more serious things once they entered the adult world. He took pride in knowing and maintaining a friendship with Bob and Abigail and their ten year old son and six year old twin daughters; they had married late and were raising a family in middle age. But they were happy and proud and content, and when he left them, he knew that he would see them again, and their connection would endure for many years to come.

From there he turned west again, through Salt Lake City, then north on Interstate 84 all the way to Oregon. Two weeks after leaving El Paso, he was in Portland, and, with a short jaunt west, he was looking out over the Pacific Ocean. He found a campground near Astoria, and settled in to living out of his truck for a final few days.

The next afternoon, he drove out to Warrenton, to Fort Stevens State Park, and walked along the trail that led to the beach and the mouth of the Columbia River as it empties into the Pacific Ocean. Here, he stood and watched the waters from the great river flowing into the even vaster ocean. As a historian, he was pulled to this seminal place in American history. Somewhere around here, he imagined, Meriwether Lewis; William Clark; Sacagawea, the Shoshoni girl who guided them all the way to the sea; and the Corps of Discovery had come to the climax of their mission in November 1805. He wondered what it was like when they beached their boats and walked on the sands bordering the ocean. They had traveled into an unknown land, faced many hardships, saw a new way to view the world, and no doubt thought of how this adventure had changed them, made them understand the greatness of life and their place in it. Neither they, nor the new nation itself, would ever be the same again. As these currents flowed through

141

his mind, he stood staring out at the ocean until the sun closeted itself behind the horizon and he walked back up to his vehicle in semi-darkness.

He visited Fort Clatsop, Lewis and Clark's winter quarters, not far away, and then, while he was in the area, drove up to Mount St. Helens. He had never been there, and the terrible majesty of the mountain with its wounded flank gave him an idea of the day in May 1980 when it erupted and forces far beyond the ken of humanity emerged to reshape the land. He walked the trails from the visitor's center along the ridges, seeing firsthand the visages of death and the new life that was shaping to take their place, took in the videos of the event, and bought some books and trinkets for his classroom. He left the area and drove back to Oregon sufficiently humbled by humanity's meager presence on Earth.

That night, he wrote in his journal, and finished it with something that his father had told him almost fifty years before, after the family had returned from a summer vacation to Canada. "Michael," the older man had said, "You'll probably travel a lot more as you get older. And the biggest experience will not be the trip itself, but when you finish it. You'll realize that at the end of each journey you'll see the world a bit more clearly." Michael closed the notebook and thought back and for the first time understood his father's words.

Epilogue

When I pulled up in the driveway and got out of the Toyota, Danae was waiting for me at the door; I had called her from Sacramento and told her I would be home in a few hours. The first thing she said was, "Dad, I may not let you in the house. You need a haircut and a shave." I had not shaved since leaving Philadelphia, and had not seen a barber since Boston in March. She watched my expression with playfulness and smiled and gave me a big hug and said, "Welcome home. But you're still going to the barbershop tomorrow. I'm not going to have a father who's beginning to look like Santa Claus." I told her, "This is from the child I helped bring forth and raised and let live in my house? I drove 3,000 miles to hear this?"

That night, Danae cooked a big dinner to celebrate my return. She invited Laura and Steve over, and, as we ate, I gave an abbreviated summary of my travels. Some of the stories they already knew from my emails, others, especially the most recent, were new, and, in many ways, enlightening to them. After dinner I set up the iPhone and took a picture of all of us together, which I sent to Elaine immediately afterwards. I had called her earlier in the day, but now I wanted her to see me with my loved ones. Fifteen minutes later, I received a reply: "You have a lovely family, but you need to get your hair cut and your beard shaved off." I showed the kids her message, and we all laughed together. Laughing as a family was something we had not done in a long time, and it felt good; it felt like living again.

The next day I drove to the hair salon I had been using ever since I came to Madera. Ray, the long-time barber who ran the place, was startled when I walked in, then grinned when he saw my hirsute growths. "Good to have you back, Michael," Ray said, and proceeded to spend the next hour returning my head and face to the state it was in before I left.

I spent my first night home sleeping in the guest room, since the master bedroom was a mess, full of clothes and shoes and books and dust, memories that I could not take care of before I left. I spent most of the next few days cleaning, changing, and moving things into the spare room. Finally for the first time in over fifteen months, I settled into the bed that Beatrice and I had shared for thirty years. It was the same bed I had always known, but it was different as well. Not just the time gone, but now I accepted the fact that Beatrice was no longer a part of it. She had shifted from being an anticipated physical presence to being a memory, a friendly ghost that inhabited the house and reminded me of what we once had together.

Shortly after I returned, I wandered around the place to study how well Danae had taken care of it. The indoors were relatively clean and organized, but it was apparent that Danae, while a good college student and fairly decent housekeeper, was no gardener. The yard needed a mowing, then extensive work on the flower beds and backyard garden. Working almost every morning for the next month, I brought the property back to life, revealing its true colors against the brown Central Valley summer.

One morning, I drove over to the Madera cemetery. I first visited Beatrice's grave, to tell her that I was safe and sound after my trip, and that I missed her. The simple light grey granite headstone, which I ordered before I left, was crisp, fresh, and gleaming among the older markers. Then I walked across to the other side of the cemetery and located my mother's resting place. Long ago, I heard an old saying: "Children initially adore their parents, then they come to judge them. Eventually, they may forgive them." I thought of my mother, and my father, too, and how they made choices that led to my siblings and eventually to myself, and the direction of their own lives as well. While someone else may have, I could not condemn my mother for what she did. Instead, I thanked her for allowing me to come into the world and experience it in all its wonder and surprise. I uttered a silent prayer that she slept peacefully, then left.

In late July I packed the Toyota with boxes of teaching supplies and books and drove over to the high school. The staff was overjoyed to see me. Barbara Winston greeted me with a big hug and warm smile as I walked into the administration office. "So, the prodigal son has returned, has he?" she commented as she looked me over.

"Have no doubt," I replied. "I always said I would be back, and I am. So there. You can't get rid of me that easily."

I received my room keys from Judith, the head secretary, and began unloading. As I pinned posters on the wall, sorted books, and perused my student rosters for the coming year, I felt as if I were slipping into well-worn and comfortable slippers, good friends, made to last a lifetime. It was good to be back in the classroom.

Danae stayed with me at the house until mid-August, then found an off-campus apartment to be shared with a classmate for her final year at Merced. She moved out on a Saturday, with myself and several of her friends helping. When I returned to the house, Charlemagne was standing by the front door yowling, wanting to look out on the street. He spent the next several days pouting around the house, refusing to eat his food, and generally announcing that he was upset over something. We found out what it was when Danae came home one night during the week to pick up some things she left in her room. At the sound of her car pulling into the driveway, Charlemagne immediately jumped up and ran to the front door. When Danae entered, he rubbed her legs and made contented sounds all the way to the kitchen, the bedroom, and the closets. As soon as Danae left, he went right back to his sullen behavior. I called her about an hour later. "I think you forgot something." "No, not that I know of." "Well, yes, you did, and he's right here." Charlemagne knew that I was talking to Danae, and was sitting next to me on the sofa, yowling as loud as he could.

The next day, after her morning classes, Danae came back, found the cat waiting for her at the door, gave him a look of both disgust and amusement, then put him in a pet carrier, and took him and the litter box and cat bed and supplies out to her car. Fortunately, the complex where she lives accepts pets. Now, she tells people, with only a little bit of embarrassment, that she has a male living with her in the apartment, and her boyfriend will have to compete with him for her time and attention.

On the first day of school, I stood outside the door greeting students who were sophomores in my world history class when I left, and were now taking AP History as seniors. I was glad to see them and they were pleased that I was back. As they walked in, I got high-fives and pats on the arm and shoulder. "Good to see you again, Mr. Lindstrom." "Great to have you back at school." The bell rang, they settled down, and I started doing what I do best: challenging them to question their assumptions and stretch themselves beyond their own immediate lives and worlds. As the school year slipped from August into September and October, they became more aware of their experiences in the class as a continuum, a process that leads and guides, for history is not a collection of dates and facts, but a living breathing entity that flows like a river through our lives. It gives us focus, guiding us to a destiny that we can shape or can shape us. It is indispensable; without it none of us would have any meaning, neither past nor future.

I come home, refreshed with energy and direction, browse through the mail, make myself dinner, then sit back and relax, read a book or magazine, or occasionally watch a television program. When I returned, I still had a good deal of cleaning to do; before I left I was almost afraid to touch some of Beatrice's clothes and personal items. For the rest of the summer, Danae, until she left, Laura, when she had the time, and I went through the things I had put in the spare bedroom, Beatrice's office, the pantry, the back patio, the shelves and boxes in the garage. The overriding mantra by Laura and Danae was, "What would Mom want us to keep?" Most of the clothes and shoes we gave to the

145

Salvation Army, her manuscripts and other papers we boxed up and put away; perhaps someday, Laura or Danae's grandchildren will want to read what their great-grandmother said about life and love at the end of the twentieth century and the beginning of the twenty-first. The few pieces of jewelry that Beatrice possessed, they divided up among themselves. The most difficult of all were the photographs; over fifty years of images that revealed the growth of a child into a young woman into a mature adult into a last testament. I was looking through the box, almost overcome, one Saturday when Laura came up to me and softly said, "Dad, I'll take care of these," and released them from my fragile hands. In late October, she came over to the house with an album, beautifully done, of the best of Beatrice in all of her evolving stages, even the last one, in the final ravages of cancer, for it was as much her as any of the others. I looked through it, and then held Laura for a long time before letting her go and saying, "Thank you."

Now, the house is very post-Beatrice; she is still there, as evidenced by the three best images that Laura chose, sitting on the mantle, in the kitchen, and on the dresser in my bedroom. Her voice, her presence is still there as well, in the furniture we bought over the years, in the dishes and silverware in the dining room, in the artwork on the walls. But it is all benign, and does not stop me from going out and buying new things and adding them to the collection that is life. So, we must go on, evolving and changing.

In early November, I received an email from Michelle Westerling. Dan was dead, from an apparent heart attack. The story went, she said, that his body was found by a maid in a motel on the outskirts of Denver. The police investigation revealed that a woman had been in the room with him, which came as no surprise to Michelle. The coroner's autopsy showed that he had large amounts of cocaine and other drugs in his system, which probably contributed to his death. With the exception of wanting to know about his financial status and her daughter's share of it, Dan's second, brief, wife had no interest in taking care of the situation, so Michelle and the boys made all the arrangements, cremating the remains and leading a small service that included only them and a few colleagues and friends. None of Dan's girlfriends or clients attended. Michelle promised to contact me if any more information came to light, but when I read her account, I quietly said grace for a man who had so much promise and ability and let it all float away as carelessly as broken leaves in the wind.

At about the same time, I sat down in my office and spent an afternoon going through my financial accounts. I ended up writing two checks and sending them back East. One was to David and Jane's daughter Martha; the other was to Susan. I explained that the money came from my parents' estate, assets that I had taken care of since their deaths, and it was only fair that they receive a portion, since they too were descendants of Stephen Lindstrom and Barbara Kessler Lindstrom of Swensen, St. Louis, and Sacramento. Martha wrote me back, gratefully saying that the money would be put into a college fund for her son. Susan returned her check, thanking me, but refusing to accept it; she felt she didn't deserve it after estranging herself from the family all those years. Whether she really meant that, or simply didn't want anything that belonged to her father and mother, I cannot venture to guess. I have since put the money into an account for her son and daughter, and they can have it when they want, or need, it.

I hear from Luz every so often. She writes that both she and Esperanza are doing well; she keeps me informed as to her educational progress. The Sorensons from Swensen have also contacted me. Samantha is graduating from high school in June, and, as a gift to her and the family, they will travel to California and visit Yosemite among other places. I wrote back saying that they are welcome to stay at my house; Yosemite Valley is only about a two hour drive away. They also say that Reverend Berg is still at the Lutheran Church, leading services every Sunday, guiding the living and comforting the sick and dying, watching over his flock. It's good to know that the community has a dedicated and eminent person to lead it.

Elaine has recently written to say that her music group has been asked to perform at a Baroque festival in Chicago during New Year's week. She hinted that it would be nice if I could come and hear them play. I have already purchased plane tickets and made arrangements to spend the entire time there with her. Denise, in our regular phone calls, keeps reminding me not to be bashful or shy about Elaine, but we are taking things patiently, and both of us will decide if, or when, the time is right.

In the meantime, I do have a companion in the house with me. When I passed through St. Louis on my way home, Carmine Rickart talked me into adopting one of her parents' dogs, a big dopy-looking and outrageously friendly chocolate lab named Ulysses. He and I took to each other immediately, and he did not even look back when we drove away from Carmine's house. He traveled west with me, sitting in the front cab, occasionally sticking his head out the passenger window, as dogs often do, and no doubt savoring the sights and smells of a new experience. Once in Madera, Charlemagne greeted him with a hiss and a swipe of his paw, and afterwards completely ignored him. Ulysses quickly accommodated himself, and is happiest chasing the squirrels in

147

the backyard. Carmine occasionally emails me and asks, among other things, how Ulysses is doing. The dog is a transplant like me, and will probably spend the rest of his days in Central California, far from his Midwest origins.

About a week ago, Laura and Steve invited me out to dinner. We met at Pardini's in Fresno, and had a sumptuous meal under candlelight. At the end, when the dishes had been cleared and we were all relaxing, Laura told me that she is pregnant, and asked that, if the child is a girl, which I suspect they already know, would it be all right to name her Beatrice. I told them that it would be nice, but they're not bound to it, and the final choice is theirs. Still, I was heartfelt that they suggested it. The baby is due in May, and when it is born it will add beauty to my contentment, a new generation coming into being, and a continuance of the lineage. I can tell Susan that I, too, know what it is like to be a grandparent.

Lately, we have had rain, for the first time in what seems like years, and the bed of the Fresno River now has a creek flowing through it. As long as the fall weather is good, Ulysses and I walk along it at dusk. Other than being occasionally bothered by gnats and mosquitos, the journey is calm and peaceful. The meandering sounds of the water ripple in my spirit. I hear the call of flickers in the distance, the rattling of a kingfisher, and every now and then the plop and splash of a frog as it jumps for a transitory view of the wider world. Overhead, a hawk circles and watches for potential meals. The leaves are turning golden hues, and the sun retreats a bit earlier each evening. Life, in all its colors, still entices. I have much more to do, much more that Beatrice would want me to do, my last pledge to her.

In the deepening sky, home is waiting for me. I call Ulysses back to my side, and we walk down the street, towards a porch light and a red Toyota truck sitting in the driveway. Somewhere down the riverbed, an owl is calling out to its mate, and is rewarded with returning hoots. I can still hear the two talking to each other as we reach the door, open it, and go inside.

About the Author

Larry Parmeter was born in San Francisco and raised in St. Louis, Missouri. After attending Centenary College of Louisiana, he moved back to California, first living in Orange County in Southern California, where he received a master's degree from Long Beach State University, and then in Northern California, where he began his teaching career. In 1989, he moved from the San Jose area to Fresno, where he presently lives. He left the high school classroom (he does not like to use the word "retired") in 2015 after over 30 years of teaching English and Social Studies. He currently works with environmental education programs for elementary school students, leads nature field trips, actively participates in amateur astronomy and space sciences, and studies martial arts as a black belt student and instructor. He and his wife Aileen have been married for 22 years; they have one son, Nathan, who is in college.